# Brother Elijah Built the Ark

# GLENIS STOTT

_CinnamonPress_

INDEPENDENT INNOVATIVE INTERNATIONAL

Published by Cinnamon Press
Meirion House
Glan yr afon
Tanygrisiau
Blaenau Ffestiniog
Gwynedd LL41 3SU
www.cinnamonpress.com

The right of Glenis Stott to be identified as author of this work has been asserted by her in accordance with the Copyright, Designs and Patent Act, 1988. © 2011 Glenis Stott. ISBN 978-1-907090-29-5
British Library Cataloguing in Publication Data. A CIP record for this book can be obtained from the British Library

Designed and typeset in Palatino and Garamond by Cinnamon Press. Cover design by Jan Fortune-Wood from original artwork by Kirk Edwards © Kirk Edwards, used with kind permission.

Printed in Poland

# Brother 'Lijah Built the Ark

# Prologue

'The Lord is my light and my salvation, whom shall I fear?'

*Oh no! Elijah's off on one again.*

'That's what Psalm twenty seven says. "The Lord is my light and my salvation." And the Lord has sent his light to shine in this room, through me, onto you. He has seen we are his special people ...'

*He gets so carried away when he starts. He does me head in.*

'...and I have been chosen to lead you. I have been chosen to be your father, your special one here on this earth, the one through whom God will channel his wishes. We cannot do wrong; we are his chosen ones...'

Liam was deep in thought as he followed the others out. George caught up with him in the corridor outside.

'How's it going Liam?'

'Oh fine, George, just fine thanks.'

Is it fine? Well, it was certainly good of them to take me in off the streets. The people are nice and the food's great. But Elijah gets me down when he goes on and on. Morning Meeting. Afternoon Assembly. Circle Time. Any excuse and he's ranting away.

And there's no space for me. What with working all day and then Social Hour and Circle Time at night, the only time I get to myself is in the bathroom. Sometimes, when I'm in bed, I'm grateful for the others' snoring; at least it lets me know no-one's going to bother me.

Not only that, there's someone watching me all the time.

*

Paul touched Liam on the shoulder, 'Are you alright Liam?'

'Yes thanks.'

Josh fell into step beside him, 'Nearly time for dinner, I'll walk down to the dining room with you.'

'I'm just going to the toilet. I'll catch up with you.'

# One

It's tough with four kids when you've nothing coming in. Joe, he's been out of work for about six months now and his drinking just gets worse and worse. I don't know what I'd do without our Liam. He's a lovely lad.

Like this morning. I'd had a bit of trouble with his dad last night. He'd been out drinking, and I was up all night with him, you know how it is. Well, I went in to our Liam and I said, 'Will you get the kids sorted for school?' and he said, 'Course I will, Mum. You go back to bed.' And he did, got them up and dressed, sorted out our Steven's bed (he wets it sometimes) and gave them their breakfast. He's only seven but he's like a proper grown-up sometimes. Bless him.

Liam stripped the bed and hung the duvet over the end of it to air before picking up the rest of the bedding and carrying it downstairs.

When he got in the yard, he dropped the duvet cover on the floor, bunched the sheet into a rope, flung the end over the washing line and pulled on the two ends until they were about even. Then he stretched the sheet out along the line until it was as straight as he could make it. When he repeated the process with the duvet cover, the weight of it meant it took three attempts to get it over the line.

It was breezy and he needed clothes pegs. He searched around and found four on the floor but he couldn't reach to clip them on. Then he had an idea. He pulled Steven's two-wheeled trike from the corner and dragged it under the washing line. He climbed on and, although it wobbled every time he reached up, he managed to secure the bedding to the line. He was breathless when he'd finished but he rushed into the kitchen to sort out breakfast.

Kirsty and Kelly were waiting at the table.

'We're hungry, Liam,' they said together

'I know, I know.'

There were three slices of bread in the bread bin and just enough margarine in the fridge to cover them.

'I want jam,' said Kelly.

'Jam, jam, jam,' said Kirsty.

Liam looked in the cupboard; the jar was on the top shelf. With practised ease, he put a chair next to the kitchen unit and climbed up on the worktop to reach the jam. Unscrewing the lid he looked inside. Not much left. He jumped down holding the jar out to the side so nothing happened to it.

Steven came into the kitchen, closing the door behind him with exaggerated care.

'Blob or spread?' asked Liam

'Blob,' said Kirsty

'Blob,' said Kelly

'Spread,' said Steven.

Liam put the knife to the bottom of the jar and scraped together a small lump of jam which he placed in the centre of one of the slices. He put another lump in the middle of a second slice and handed the twins one each. Grinning in delight they began to nibble round the edges of the bread, working their way to the treat in the centre.

Liam looked back in the jar. He worked his way round with the knife and spread a thin layer for Steven's slice of bread.

'Aren't you having any breakfast, Liam?'

'Not hungry.'

There was silence while Liam poured four glasses of water and set them on the table. He sat down and watched them eating.

'Kirsty, what are you doing?'

'She's got a bit of jam on her nose; I'm licking it off for her.'

They both giggled. Liam and Steven looked at each other.

'Yuk,' they said together

# Two

Dinner was the usual noisy event, everyone chattering about their day. Three long tables, about twenty people to each table, sitting so close together that no one could leave without the active co-operation of the people either side. Dishes were passed up and down continuously and it was wise to keep an eye open for the occasional misplaced elbow. There was quiche, ham, turkey, salad from the garden and home baked bread. When all the plates were empty, there was the best apple pie Liam had ever tasted, along with thick sweet custard.

After dinner, Liam followed the others to Circle Time but, luckily, he did not have to actively participate that evening so he semi-dozed through Paul's talk, feeling grateful for his pleasantly full stomach.

*Social Hour, 8.00 pm*

The soon-to-disappear sun lit the large space created by pulling back the partition between the Morning Room and Dining Room. People sat, sprawled and lay on non-matching ageing sofas and chairs at one end of the room, benches and tables at the other. Everyone was there to relax and socialise after a long day cooking, cleaning and caring for the forty-eight members of The Community, plus doing the renovation and maintenance demanded by the large dilapidated house.

Liam was on one of the benches, playing a game with Becky who was sitting nearby on Rebecca's knee. She had celebrated her first birthday the week before and had a vocabulary of three words: 'Mummum', 'Lijah' and

'Peep'. She covered her face with her hands then pulled them away shouting, 'Peep' as loudly as she could. Liam was laughingly doing the same when Josh came in and disturbed them.

'Alright room-mate?'

Tom and Ian followed and sat opposite.

Liam buried his head in his hands and growled, 'Isn't it bad enough I have to work with you *and* share a room with you without having to sit with you at Social Hour?' The other three said, 'It's a hard life!' in unison, and then high-fived around Liam's bowed head.

The door opened again and Paul came in with his guitar. The room quietened as Paul settled down at the end farthest from Liam. He asked what they wanted to start with and Rebecca's voice was the loudest with 'Michael Row the Boat Ashore.' Paul led the singing and Tom drummed a rhythm on the tabletop, not always matching the singing, but no-one minded.

The next request was for 'Up at the Larches.' Paul sang the verses and everyone joined in for 'Up at The Larches.' Liam wished he was somewhere else.

We're all part
Of one big family
Up at The Larches
Up at The Larches

We work and we play
We sing and we pray
Up at The Larches
Up at The Larches

I care for you
And you care for me
Up at The Larches
Up at The Larches

Now here is someone
I want to you to meet
Up at The Larches
Up at The Larches

Paul pointed to Liam who dragged himself to his feet to sing:

My name is Liam
And I'm new here
Up at The Larches
Up at The Larches

Already I feel
Quite at home here
Up at The Larches
Up at The Larches

Liam sat down and Paul pointed to the new members one by one. There was loud applause at the end, with several calls for an encore but, thankfully, Paul moved on to 'Kum By Yah.'

Becky, supported by the arm of her mother's chair, danced to the music, bending her knees, stretching up on to her toes and grinning widely. The door opened; she shouted, "Lijah!' and let go of the chair, stretching out her arms before taking first one step and then another towards him. Rebecca yelled, 'Becky's walking', Paul stopped playing and everyone was silent as they watched her progress.

The last rays of the sun touched the back of Becky's head, turning her hair into a golden halo. Elijah crouched down and said, 'Come on Becky'. She put her arms out to the side to keep her balance and, with the careful attention of a tightrope walker, made her way towards him, taking the last few steps at an almost-run and staggering straight into his arms. Elijah picked her up and swung her round, making her giggle, before lifting her on his shoulder and carrying her on a lap of honour round the room. There were cheers and clapping as Paul began to sing:

Our Becky
Has learnt to walk
Up at The Larches
Up at The Larches.

# Three

Liam Donnelly? Yes he's in my class. Nice little boy, although the family seem to have a lot of problems. Dad was unemployed for quite a long time and Mum struggles to cope both financially and with the demands of four young children.

Liam's a good little worker and keen to be friends with everyone but, to be honest, he's not the cleanest child in the class. On a couple of occasions I've found him a change of clothing and taken him into the toilets for a wash. You have to do it sometimes, the other children complain about the smell. Not that I'm blaming Liam of course. From the things he's told me, he's the most responsible person in that household. He gets the others up most mornings, gives them their breakfast and makes sure they get to school. It's sad but what can you do?

Miss Moorhouse, the head, was taking assembly. She was nice, but a bit scary.

'Let's say a prayer, just to ourselves, about our own family. Think of the things you like about your family and say thank you to God for them.'

Liam closed his eyes and put his hands together. *Thank you, God, for Mum and Steven and Kirsty and Kelly. Thank you for the fun we have when we're playing in the bedroom. Thank you for when Mum makes Shepherd's Pie for tea.* He opened his eyes. Then he remembered something else. He screwed his eyes up tight and pressed his hands so tightly together that they shook. *Please, please, please let Dad keep his new job so that Mum's happy.*

As they were walking out of the hall Liam twisted his shoes on the polished floor to make them squeak. That was his happy noise. His friend Gareth was behind him. He nudged Liam and then made his shoes squeak as well.

The two giggled. They squeaked and squeaked their shoes as much as possible.

'Liam and Gareth. What *are* you doing?'

'Nothing, Miss Moorhouse.'

Back in the classroom, Mrs Watson asked the class to draw a picture of their family. Liam liked drawing. His tongue stuck out of his mouth as he pressed the stubby wax crayons on the pink paper. He'd lost his yellow crayon so he had to borrow Gareth's to do Mum's hair and the sun. He took it out to the front to show Mrs Watson.

'That's lovely, Liam. Are you going to tell me who everyone is?'

'That's my Mum in the middle. She's called Margaret but Dad calls her Mags. That's me next to her, then Steven.'

'He's in Class three, isn't he?'

'Yes Miss. Kirsty and Kelly, the twins are on her other side. They're in Class one.'

'Who's that over there in the corner?'

'That's my Dad, Miss. He's called Joe.'


When he was leaving the classroom to go home, Mrs Watson said, 'Liam you look happy tonight'

'I am, Miss, we're going swimming and then we're going to McDonalds and Mum says I can have a Big Mac and a milk shake'

'You're a lucky boy.'

'I know, Miss and you know what?'

'What?'

'We might be going a lot now Dad's got a new job.'

'That's good, Liam, that's really good'

*

Liam stretched his mouth wide round the Big Mac and then bit down. Hard. Then he sucked and sucked on his straw to force the chocolate milk shake up the straw. His ears popped.

'Mum can we go to America?'

'Why do you want to go to America?'

'They drink milk shakes and eat burgers all the time there.'

'No, Liam, we can't afford to go to America even with Dad's new job but I might be able to buy you some new pyjamas next week.'

After McDonalds they went with Mum to choose a new lamp. They bought the one that Liam liked best. A red base with a yellowy coloured shade which had little red flowers along the edge. It was the most beautiful one in the shop.

It was cold when they were walking home but once inside the house they were soon warm. Liam persuaded Mum to plug the new lamp in to test it and turned off the big light so they all could admire it.

'It makes the settee look like an island in the middle of a black sea,' Steven said.

Liam wished he'd said that and made his mum smile.

Kirsty and Kelly were so tired they actually asked to go to bed and Steven couldn't keep his eyes open so Mum made him go upstairs as well. That left Liam and Mum. They sat and watched television in their cosy lamplit island. There was a sitcom that made them both laugh out loud and a quiz show they could shout the answers at. Next a man talked to another man about his new film but Liam couldn't understand what they were saying so he leant against Mum and closed his eyes. She lifted her arm and put it around his shoulders, pulling him into her circle of warmth.

He was in America buying the biggest chocolatiest milk shake ever in a McDonalds' school hall run by Mrs Watson. He put the cup on a boat shaped table and sat down, waving at Mrs Watson as he floated past her.

A big seal jumped up on the boat table and made it rock.

'I've got a job for you, Mags.'

The seal in the water said 'No, Joe, not now. Liam's here, wait, please wait.'

The big seal clapped his fins. 'I said I've got a job for you! Get rid of him or I'll make him go and you'll both be sorry.'

The seals and the boat disappeared.

'Liam, Liam, go upstairs. Get to bed now!'

That was mum's scared voice. Only partly awake, Liam rolled off the settee onto the floor. He scrambled up and made his way to the door where he turned back to look at Mum and Dad.

'Liam, go on. Hurry up.' Mum said.

In bed he curled up as small as he could and tried to sleep but all he could do was wonder why Dad's willy had been so big.

# Four

Elijah was waiting for them in the Assembly Room, resting against a small table and holding a marker pen between thumb and forefinger. Liam, Gemma, Ruth, Tom and Pat seated themselves on the five chairs forming a circle in front of him. As he watched them settle, Elijah pressed one end of the pen against his other palm, then slid his thumb and forefinger down to the end before turning it upside down to repeat the process. His 'Ready?' resulted in everyone nodding and then some rustling as they made themselves comfortable.

'We're going to talk about sin tonight. I've got a list of the Seven Deadly Sins here. I know they seem a bit old-fashioned but it's just a way for us to start the discussion.' He held up a sheet of flipchart paper. 'What I want us to do first is produce a definition of each one of these sins. Anyone want to be scribe?'

Everyone looked at the floor but eventually Gemma held her hand out for the pen. 'Go on then, I'll do it.'

Kneeling on the floor with the piece of paper in front of her, she summarised the group's words on the flipchart at the end of each discussion. When they'd finished, Elijah pinned it on the flipchart stand.

7 Deadly Sins

Pride
Needing to be superior to others

Covetousness
Longing for something especially if it belongs to someone else

Lust
Unhealthily wanting someone or something

Envy
Resenting someone else's success

Gluttony
Eating too much or wanting to eat too much

Anger
Strong emotion caused by something that you don't agree with

Sloth
Being lazy

'Right. Now we've got a definition of all these sins, let's have a look at what they have in common.'

Liam was peering through a schoolroom fog as Ruth leant forward.

'A lot of them are to do with needing and wanting things. To look good, to have possessions, to have people agree with you, to eat a lot, to be successful. I'm not sure about sloth though.'

'I think you're right,' said Elijah. 'They are about wanting things. Even sloth is about wanting, in a way. It's about wanting to do as little as possible. Elijah looked round the group. 'So what's wrong with wanting things?'

Gemma had the answer. 'It's selfish.'

Elijah nodded. 'It is selfish to always be wanting things. Particularly in a community like this one.'

Gemma looked up at Elijah. She smiled. 'In a community you need to think about the others all the time.'

'That's right. We're a team. That means we have to make decisions about what is and isn't important on a daily basis. What's important here at The Larches?'

'Talking to people about God.'

'Looking after the children.'

'Caring for each other.'

'Prayer.'

Elijah held up his hand for them to stop before Liam had found any answers.

'It's a long list. How can we sum it up?'

After a pause Tom said, 'The important thing at The Larches is to put the community first and ourselves second.'

Everyone nodded. Even Liam could see the point of that. Elijah made a move towards the flipchart.

'If I wrote a list of priorities on this board, does everyone agree that Number One would be The Community and Number Two would be each individual person?'

Everyone stared at Elijah. It wasn't only Liam who looked puzzled this time. Only Ruth had the courage to speak.

'But what about God?'

'Good point, Ruth. That's why we're all here, because of God. It would be very selfish to put The Community above God. How about this?'

Priorities

1. God
2. The Community
3. The Individual

'That's better,' said Tom.

'You might think we've come a long way from talking about Sin. But we haven't really. Let's go back to what we said about the Seven Deadly Sins. We said that they were all about being selfish, about wanting things for ourselves.'

Elijah put down his pen and walked round the back of the group where he stood and read out the list of priorities. 'One - God. Two - The Community. Three - The Individual. If we truly follow those priorities, do you think it would be possible to be selfish? Could we be guilty of any sin? '

There was a silence. Elijah squeezed through the gap in two chairs and walked back to the chart.

His voice was louder. 'I think if we follow these priorities there is no possibility of us sinning. Whatever is right for God and The Community cannot be a sin.'

Elijah turned to the next, already completed, flipchart sheet. 'What do you think of this?'

The Community's Definition of Sin

Putting your needs and wants above those of God and The Community

Liam's fog grew thicker. He thought they'd been working things out between them yet Elijah seemed to have the answers planned out already.

'You're right, Elijah. That's all we need.' Gemma put down her pen amidst lots of smiles and nods.

Elijah said, 'One final point. There's a question I'm often asked. Why don't we accept couples? This is the reason. When a couple have committed to each other in the outside world they would come into The Community with a history of putting each other first. However hard they tried it would be too difficult to put that history behind them. Does that make sense?'

Gemma and Ruth replied together. 'It does.'

Tom and Pat murmured agreement. Liam didn't say anything. His fog had almost solidified; he could neither see where he was nor how he'd got there.

'Okay. That's about it for tonight's discussion. Let's end with a short prayer.'

Elijah raised his arms and looked up at the ceiling. 'Lord, give us the strength to carry out thy work. We've set ourselves a big task but the Lord will make us strong. Together we can save the world. Amen'

The group linked hands and raised their arms into the air. 'Praise the Lord.'

When they left the Assembly Room, Liam told the others he needed some fresh air. What he actually needed was a drink but he kept that to himself. He sat on the top step outside the front door and looked down at the lights of Burnley spread out below him. A long time ago that had been his home; a place where he had done his best to care for his brother and sisters. And his mother. Now it all felt as if it had happened to someone else.

The front door opened behind him. It was Tom.

'Hi, Liam. Thought you were out here. We were thinking of skipping Social Hour and having an early night. We're all shattered but we'd like another early start tomorrow. What do you think?'

Elijah had asked the four room-mates to clear out the old barn. They'd been up at six and worked all day long but there was still a lot to do.

'I think that's a good idea. I'll be up in a minute.'

Tom went back inside as Liam stood and gazed again at the lights, wondering where his brother and sisters were. The last time he'd seen them they'd been in foster care but, after all this time, he was sure they must have moved away from the area. He turned and went inside. As he reached the bottom of the stairs, Elijah was coming down.

'Not going to Social Hour?'

'Not tonight. Having an early night.'

'Hmm.'

# Five

Me and Mags had to get married because of Liam - she got caught first time we did it. Typical. Then she gets caught the year after with Steven and then the year after that with twins. Twins. Bloody stupid woman. So I takes her down to the clinic to get sorted. She has injections now. Whinges because they make her arm sore. I says to her, 'Better than another set of twins, int'it?'

She's always whingeing about something. Washer's broke. Twins need new shoes. And she was always on at me to get a job. 'Get a job, Joe. Get a job.' So I gets a job and a right nightmare it turns out to be. Labouring. How can you hold your head up when you're digging holes for a living? I hate it. And they know it. Every so often some bloke in a suit comes to me and says 'Joe, this is your final warning. One more misdemeanour and you're out.' Misdemeanour, I ask you. Must've swallowed a bloody dictionary.

Get a bit of peace when I hand the money over. But then she starts again. Says it's not enough. Complains about me spending some down at the pub … a bloke's got to have his drinking money, hasn't he? She seems to do alright from it anyway, bought herself a new lamp the other day.

Anyway, she's persuaded me to take her and the kids to Blackpool for the day. I've said I'll go but we have to be back before the pubs close. It might keep her mouth shut for a while.

When they left the train station Dad bought a bucket and spade for them to share.

Mum and Dad sat on the prom watching as the boys ran down on to the sands. Liam and Steven began to build a big sandcastle. Steven wanted to use the spade to dig but that was alright with Liam; he liked to feel the sand with his hands. The twins used the bucket to bring seawater for the moat. It was a long way to the sea and each time they brought a new bucketful they found the first had disappeared.

After a while Dad shouted for Liam. Liam walked towards him quite slowly; he thought he might be in trouble.

'Come on Liam, hurry up, we're going to the chippy for some dinner. I need someone to help me carry everything.'

Dad held Liam's hand as they crossed the road; he said the trams were dangerous. Liam could hear them roaring in the distance and he was glad Dad was holding his hand.

In the chippy Liam's feet squeaked on the floor. He laughed. Dad smiled and made his feet squeak as well. Then they squeaked their feet together. The happiness ballooned up inside Liam so it filled him from his sand covered toes right up to the brown curls on the top of his head.

On the way back Dad said, 'Where do you want to go when we've eaten? The Pleasure Beach? A ride on a tram? Blackpool Tower?'

'Pleasure Beach please.'

'That's funny, that's just where I wanted to go.'

The salty sand on Liam's fingers mixed with the taste of the fish and chips and it was delicious. When Liam and Steven had finished their shared tray there was a pool of vinegar in the bottom. They fought over who was to lick it up. Liam won.

Then the Pleasure Beach. People. Noise. Lights. Rides. Ice cream. Slot machines. Smells. Hot dogs. More rides. Candy floss. Steven was sick. Twice. It was great.

It was late when they got on the train. Kirsty and Kelly sat either side of Dad and went to sleep while Liam and Steven took turns spelling out the names of the stations.

'Curly Kuh, huh, eh, ruh, ruh, yuh. What's that?' said Steven.

'It's Cherry stupid! Cherry Tree.'

'I'm not stupid!'

'Are too.'

'Am not.'

'Now boys, don't spoil a lovely day. Don't you think Cherry Tree's a nice name? Wouldn't you like to live somewhere with a name like that?'

'If you were there, Mum,' said Liam.

When they got home Mum made them have a bath to get rid of the sand. Then they put on their new pyjamas and got in bed where Liam felt so warm and snuggly it didn't take long for him to go to sleep.

Later on he woke and went to the toilet. He could hear Mum and Dad shouting downstairs, then Mum screamed.

'Joe, stop. I'm sorry.' She gasped. 'Please, please. Leave me alone.'

Liam crept to the top of the stairs and looked down. Mum and Dad were standing just outside the front room door.

Dad said, 'You stupid bitch,' and grabbed hold of Mum's hair. When he raised his other arm, Liam, not thinking, ran downstairs and tried to grab it so he wouldn't hit Mum again.

'Don't, Dad. Leave her alone.'

Dad let go of Mum and turned towards Liam.

26

'So you want to protect your Mum, do you? I'll show you, you little bastard.'

Mum said 'Run, Liam. I'll be okay.'

Liam started to run up the stairs to get away from Dad but Dad reached through the spindles and caught him. Mum must have dug her nails into Dad's arm to make him let go because Dad pulled his hand back through the rails and hit mum across the face. She fell backwards against the wall, banging her head. She managed to pull herself upwards but then overbalanced and fell the other way, against the banister, hitting her head again. She swayed, trying to hold herself upright but collapsed on the floor, across the hallway. Liam stood still for a moment and then ran to her. He had to climb over her to see her face and he was shocked to see a trickle of blood running down her forehead.

'Mum, Mum, are you okay?' She moaned.

Dad said, 'Leave her. She'll be alright in a minute. You get to bed out of my sight.'

Liam didn't want to leave Mum, but Dad was so angry and Mum couldn't help him this time. He went slowly up the stairs and climbed into bed. He couldn't get comfortable. He felt cold and shivery and Kirsty was snoring. He tried to sleep, he really did, but he couldn't.

After about an hour he crept back downstairs. She was still there. On the floor. He stroked her head and when he took his hand away it was red and sticky. The light was on in the kitchen. He took a deep breath and went in. Dad was at the table.

'Dad, Mum hasn't got up. I think she's hurt.'

'I told you. She'll be right. Get back to bed before I knock the living daylights out of you.' Dad didn't sound angry anymore, just very tired.

Liam backed away but was determined to get help for his Mum. 'Dad, please come and look at her, she might need a doctor.'

Dad got up from his chair and aimed a blow at Liam's head. Liam ducked and ran back to Mum. He knelt down next to her. 'Look, she's bleeding.'

Dad stood over Mum. 'Get up, Mags.'

She didn't move. He tried to pull her up by her arm. Her shoulder lifted off the floor but that made her head loll backwards. He let go of her hand quickly and her head crashed on to the floor. He looked down at her for a moment and then turned to Liam.

'Tell you what, Liam, I'll go and get a doctor for her.'

Dad was going to sort it out. Dad pulled his coat down from the hook and put it on. He looked at Liam in a funny way then he grabbed hold of Liam by the front of his pyjamas and lifted him until Liam's eyes were level with his.

'This was all your fault. If you ever, ever tell anyone what happened they'll send you to prison. You tell them she fell down the stairs. Understand?'

'I won't never tell nobody.'

Dad lowered him and stepped over Mum. He opened the front door and turned back.

'Remember, Liam, keep your bloody mouth shut.'

Then he was gone. It was very quiet without Dad. And a little bit scary. Liam ran upstairs and pulled the pillow and quilt from Mum and Dad's bed. He struggled downstairs with them, put the pillow under Mum's head and covered her with the quilt. Remembering what Mrs Watson had done when he cut his knee, he went to get a cloth and some water to clean Mum's cut head but he couldn't find one so he got some paper towel and wet it under the tap. When he wiped away the blood the paper towel broke up and left little white bits in the stickiest part of the cut. After he'd cleaned it as well as he could, he went back into the kitchen, climbed on the worktop and found the plasters in the cupboard. They were much too small for the cut but he used three to cover up the worst bit. Then he sat down beside Mum and stroked her hand.

'Don't worry, Mum. Dad's gone for the doctor.'

Several times he got up and went into the front room to peer through the window. No sign of Dad. Mum seemed to be getting colder so Liam cuddled up to her to try and warm her with his body. She must have been fast asleep because she didn't snuggle back like she usually did.

Then it seemed to be lighter in the hallway. He stood up and crossed the front room to look out of the window again. It was daylight outside but there was still no sign of Dad. Liam climbed gingerly over Mum and went upstairs to his bedroom. He bent over Steven's bed.

'Steven, Steven. Wake up, wake up,' he whispered.

Steven opened his eyes and jumped.

'Liam, you've got blood all over your pyjamas. Are you hurt?'

'Sh. Not so loud, you'll wake the twins. Mum's hurt, she's at the bottom of the stairs. Dad went to get a doctor, but he mustn't be able to find one 'cos he hasn't come back. I can't think what to do.'

Steven climbed out of bed and they both went downstairs; Liam felt so much better now that there was someone else with him.

Steven said, 'Should we go next door for Mrs Rushton?'

'No, she'll shout.'

Steven shook his head. 'She always shouts.'

They sat thinking.

'I know. Mrs Watson said if ever anyone was hurt then we should ring 999 for an ambulance.'

'But the phone doesn't work anymore, Liam'.

'I know. We'll go to the phone box'.

They found Mum's purse and took some money out to pay for the phone. When they got there they didn't know what to do with the money, but it worked without.

'We want an ambulance. Mum's fallen down the stairs.'

'I need to ask you some questions. Can you tell me your name?'

'It's Liam. Liam Donnelly.'

'What's your address, Liam?'

'36 Jacob Street. Mum's hurt. Can you help her?'

'We're sending someone now. Who else is there?'

'Me and Steven are in the phone box. The twins are still in bed.'

'Are there any grown-ups around, Liam?'

'Dad went to get a doctor last night but he didn't come back. I think he couldn't find one.'

'Okay. Don't worry. Everything's going to be okay. The ambulance will be there very soon. You and Steven go back to the house, tell Mum it's on its way.'

'We will.'

Liam and Steven went back to the house.

Liam said, 'Don't worry, Mum. The ambulance will be here soon.'

Mum didn't say anything. The two boys sat on the stairs facing the open front door so they could see when the ambulance got there. It arrived followed by a police car. The ambulance men came to the front door.

One of them said, 'Oh my God. Get these kids out of here.'

'Come on kids, let's you get you outside.'

Kirsty and Kelly appeared at the top of the stairs. The other ambulance man looked up at them.

'It's okay. Nothing to worry about.'

The twins walked downstairs holding hands and the ambulance man ushered the four of them out on to the street. He looked at the police car and shook his head, then went back inside.

A lady policeman got out of the police car. She came over to the boys.

'Hiya, my name's Debbie. Which one of you is Liam?'

Liam stepped forward. 'That's me.'

'You did a good job ringing 999. You were very brave.'

'Steven was with me. Kirsty and Kelly were still asleep, they've just woken up.'

Another policeman got out of the car.

'Debbie, do you want to put the kids in the car while I have a look?'

Debbie opened the back door and the children climbed in. Debbie sat in the front and turned round to talk to them.

'Who else lives in your house?'

'Just Dad, he went to find a doctor but he didn't come back.'

The policeman came back to the car.

'Now this is a really important question. Did you move your Mum after she fell?'

Liam thought hard. 'I put a pillow under her head and covered her with the quilt. Oh and before that Dad pulled on her arm to try to make her get up but that just moved her head a bit.'

The policeman nodded. 'Right. Debbie, take these boys to the station. I'll radio through for a Social Worker.'

The police station had a shiny floor. Liam's shoes squeaked when he walked but it didn't make him happy.

Debbie said she'd clean Liam up. She lifted him up to sit on the worktop. She dampened a paper towel under the tap and began to wipe off the blood. The water made the towel break up and little bits of white paper stuck in the blood on Liam's arm. Liam started to sob.

'Are you going to send me to prison?'

'Why would I do that, Liam? You haven't done anything wrong.'

'Dad said … Dad said …'

'What did Dad say?'

'Nothing. He didn't say nothing.'

Then he was sick. All over Debbie's uniform.

# Six

Thank God they've gone to sleep, bit of peace and quiet. Could probably do with sleeping myself but need to do some thinking. What did Elijah mean by 'Hmm'? Was he telling me off? Should I feel guilty, like skiving off school?

It wasn't my idea. Tom suggested it. Not only that, you're allowed to miss one, it's only when you miss three you have to talk to a Leader. So what was he on about, hmming at me? He doesn't half go on about things, lecturing us in Assembly, quoting the Bible, calling himself the Son of God. I don't understand it, why do they all think he's so bloody wonderful, running round after him, holding on to every word he says. I don't get it.

It's not only Elijah I don't understand. It's everything. Everyone else always has the right answers, know why things are done the way they are. It's like secondary school where everyone knew the rules except me. I didn't know the answers in class then either.

I shouldn't be here; I don't fit in and never will. I've gotta get out. But how? Not the front door, too near the office, too near Elijah and the Leader. Kitchen door? No, kitchen's never empty, always someone cooking or washing up. God the food's good here. Have to keep my eyes open, look for a way out.

*Thursday 2.00 pm, the grounds of The Larches*

Liam spotted an opportunity and made a plan. Up to the kitchen garden, leave the wheelbarrow in the shed, double back through the trees and over the wall at the

33

back of the house. He forced himself to be casual so no one would suspect.

When he was within sight of the back wall he saw Jess. She strolled towards him. 'Hiya, Liam! I'm taking a break from the kitchen. It drives me crazy!'

He smiled. 'I know what you mean'.

Silence.

'What are you doing?'

Liam looked at the ground. He couldn't think—the noise from the wind in the trees was deafening him. 'I'm trying to escape,' he said.

'You don't need to *escape*. You could just leave. We'd discuss it with you certainly, but, if you really wanted to go no-one would try to stop you.'

'I didn't think it was as easy as that.'

Jess sat down on the grass and patted the ground next to her. 'Let's talk about it.'

Liam hesitated and then sat beside her, hugging his knees and looking everywhere except at Jess.

'What are you escaping from?'

'Lots of things really. Being watched all the time. Elijah's ranting and raving. Feeling like I'm back in school.'

Jess bent her head towards him, trying to catch his eye. 'Is there anything you do like?'

He turned to look at her. 'Most of the people, especially my room mates. The food. Working outdoors. The house is nice as well; I've never been in a house as big as this before.'

'So it's not all bad?'

'Oh no, it's not all bad. But every time I move there's someone asking what I'm doing or if I'm alright.'

'We don't *watch* each other Liam. Everyone cares for everyone else so they like to make sure you're alright, especially when someone is as new as you.'

'Alright then, what about Elijah and this son of God stuff?'

The sun shone through the leaves, casting changing patterns of light and shade across their faces. The wind played with Jess's hair. A stray hair caught on her lip. She pulled it away before speaking.

'Elijah's a very special man. He does believe that he's the son of God but only in the way that we're all God's children.'

Liam picked at a tuft of grass. 'He's given me the creeps since I first met him.'

Jess looked thoughtful. 'Tell you what; have you ever been up on the hill to look over The Larches and its grounds?'

'No, I've just seen the kitchen garden and the bit around the barn.'

'There's a gate down here, I've got the key, let's go and have a look.'

Jess unlocked the gate and led him up a path through trees that must have been there forever. At the top of the path she turned left and crossed the grass to the fence. Liam followed her.

Pointing as she spoke, she told him, 'The grounds go almost as far as the church steeple that way and right down to the stream in the other direction.'

'Wow. It's enormous.'

'It is big, isn't it? It has quite a history to it as well. A family home, a boarding school, a hotel and then converted back to a family home again.'

'A house this size for just one family? How did The Community come to own it?'

'We were lucky, in a way. A much-treasured member died and left it to us. Her name was Amy and we miss her a lot. It was in a bad state though; we're doing it up gradually.'

He nodded. 'What about money? I haven't claimed any benefits since I got here. How can you afford to support people like me?'

Jess seemed surprised at his question. 'Oh, I forgot, you missed the induction workshop didn't you?'

Liam looked embarrassed. 'Yeah, I was busy drying out at the time.'

Jess patted his shoulder. 'These things happen. Well, Elijah likes us to be self-sufficient. When members make their six-month commitment they sign over their assets. We manage but it can be a struggle. We're hoping to build up a small catering business when the kitchen extension's ready. Oh and there's Paul's website design company.'

Liam grimaced. 'Computers! Not my thing at all.'

'What is your thing, Liam?'

'Gardening. I love it.' He pointed to a large overgrown patch some distance from the house. 'Wouldn't mind having a go at that.'

'Won't get a chance to do that if you leave though, will you?'

'No, suppose not.'

Liam stared off into the distance. He chopped. He pruned. He weeded. He dug. And he planted. Then he turned his gaze to Jess. 'What are you into, Jess?'

The wind blew Jess's hair over her face again. She tucked it back behind her ears in an automatic gesture. 'I love being a Leader. It seems strange now but when I came here I was really shy. I couldn't look anyone in the face, never mind speak to them. Now I take Morning Meeting, allocate jobs; even tell others off if their work doesn't come up to scratch. The Community can make a big difference to people's lives.'

'That's what Rebecca says.'

'Oh yes, we've definitely helped Rebecca. She had no idea how to care for little Becky after she was born.

When Paul asked them to come and visit us they were both in a pitiful condition, unclean and under-nourished. Becky cried constantly and Rebecca couldn't cope.'

'They're not like that now.' Liam laughed. 'It was great when Becky started walking the other night.'

Jess smiled. 'It was, wasn't it?'

They leant against the fence and looked down on The Larches snuggling securely against its green patchwork quilt. Bright T-shirts danced with faded jeans on the washing line. Children's laughter floated up on the wind.

'Are you going to give us another chance, Liam?'

The trees nodded and yessssed around him. 'I'll give it a go.'

They heard the Afternoon Assembly gong in the distance. 'We'd better go,' said Jess.

As they approached the house Liam thought he saw Elijah watching them through the window but when he looked again there was no-one there.


*Morning Meeting, Friday*

Liam was on the second row, next to Jess. Everyone, apart from Elijah, was there. There was lots of chatter but that ended when Elijah came in. He slammed the door and threw his clipboard down on the table. His voice was shaky when he spoke. 'This morning I have a very serious task. One of our members has let us down. Neglected their duties.'

Like everyone else, Liam looked round, trying to guess who the culprit was.

'Not only that, it was a Leader. She left the kitchen yesterday afternoon and it was only because the others doubled their efforts that we had an evening meal.'

Liam stared at Elijah in amazement.

'I'd like that person to come out to the front so that we can all see who it is.'

Anger bubbled up in Liam. It wasn't fair. He began to stand but Jess put a hand on his shoulder and whispered, 'Don't, you'll only make it worse.'

Liam sat back down, adrenalin flowing with nowhere to go, body tense, nails digging into the palms of his hands, toes curled inside his shoes. Jess walked to the front and stood before Elijah. Her neck curved down as if her head was too heavy.

'Have you anything to say?'

Jess lifted her head to look in his eyes, then she shook it from side to side before dropping it down again. Liam bit his lip till it hurt.

'I choose my Leaders for their reliability. What were you thinking when you left your duties? Did you not realise what problems it would cause?'

Liam hated to see Jess humiliated like that. Especially when it was his fault. He felt tears of impotence in his eyes.

'I want you to stand down as Leader until you can prove to me that you are worthy of such an honour! Now go and sit back down.'

As she returned to her seat, head still bowed, Liam saw a tear glinting on the curve of her cheek. He longed to wipe it away then hold and comfort her. But he couldn't. He knew that. He tucked his shaking hands under his legs to keep them under control.

Elijah turned to his audience.

'This is a special community. We are *all* carrying out God's work, whether it's going into towns and cities spreading the word, cooking a meal, caring for the children or even washing the dishes. We're like a machine; every cog needs to turn in order for us to function. When someone puts themselves first and doesn't do their allocated job, that person lets us all down. It's important that we think about that and try even harder to give all we have each and every day.'

The room was silent as Elijah swept his gaze along the rows. Liam didn't see Elijah's look or hear the silence. He was inside himself, nerves and muscles on alert for ways to help Jess.

'Now on to happier things. The Lord gave flowers to the world to bring joy and colour into our lives. We have so much land we could give over to cultivate them. This is a God given way we could bring in funds to help our community grow. '

The words took light years to reach Liam's consciousness and only gained entry because of 'flowers' and 'land'.

'There's a patch of land that would be perfect. It's overgrown and full of rubbish just now but, with work, it just fits the bill. Unfortunately the building of the kitchen extension means that we're a bit short of manpower at the moment, but I thought a couple of people could make a start.' Elijah looked around.

'Liam, what about you? You used to be a gardener didn't you?'

Liam agreed automatically.

'We'd need someone who knows what they're doing to look after this project. Would you be interested?'

An emotional thunderstorm threatened to overtake Liam. The rumblings of anger, rage and frustration were joined by a lightning flash of opportunity.

'Yes.'

Elijah continued, 'How about taking Jess under your wing, you'll be able to keep an eye on her, make sure she doesn't go wandering off again?'

The words washed over Liam. He was on emotional overload, but he seemed to have made a response as Elijah said, 'Good that's sorted. I'll talk to you about it later.'

*

Liam and Jess stood side by side looking at the wilderness that was going to be a garden. 'We've got our work cut out here, Jess.'

She looked up into his face and smiled. 'Anything's better than that kitchen.'

# Seven

Sometimes I think I'm too soft to be a Social Worker. When I saw Liam at the police station that day I wanted to scoop him up and take him home with me. He looked so tiny and vulnerable. The police had taken his pyjamas away to send to forensics. They'd found him this enormous old T-shirt—the sleeves came down over his hands, the hem right to his ankles. Poor little thing.

The other three didn't seem to have realised what was happening. The twins chatted to each other quite happily and Steven was drawing a picture of a car. But Liam! He understood that something terrible had happened, even though he wasn't old enough to truly understand the impact that the events of that night would have on his life. His skin gradually took on a grey-green pallor and he kept blinking as if to make it all go away.

The police were very gentle when questioning him, both that day and on later occasions. Still, however gentle they were, there was no denying that Liam had to talk about some very traumatic issues. He was determined to protect his Dad, to stick to his story that Mum had fallen down the stairs. Of course, the police knew that wasn't true, it was obvious from the position of the body.

Eventually, Liam broke down. At first he said it was all his fault, that he'd made his Mum fall and bang her head. At one stage he even said that his Dad wasn't there, that he hadn't come back from the pub. The truth came out gradually over the course of several weeks of interviews and the police pieced together a valid description of the incident.

The children were put into foster care. We were lucky enough to have a foster carer who could take all four of them together. And she could keep them too, rather than move them on somewhere else. To be honest, she wouldn't have been my first choice for these particular children, but sometimes you have to take what's available.

'Liam, can I get in your bed?'

'Course you can.'

Steven tiptoed across the dark room and climbed in.

'Do you think Kirsty and Kelly are alright in that other room? I wish we could all sleep together.'

'Me too. That foster lady's mean.'

'No she's not, Liam. She's nice. And she says we have to call her Auntie Mary.'

'She's not our auntie. Aunties are people who are related or friends of your Mum and Dad. Do you remember Auntie Liz who was Mum's friend when we lived on Holland Street? She was really nice.'

Steven took hold of Liam's hand.

'We're not going to see Mum again are we?'

'No. She's dead, Steven.'

# Eight

They began in the far corner of the plot and, working side by side, they cleared a small patch at a time. As the days went by they became closer; sometimes they talked whilst they were working, sometimes they remained silent in the way that only close companions can.

Most of the days were hot but one cool dull day they made a bonfire just before lunch and sat down to eat within the range of its comforting flames. The firelight reflected on the foil as Jess made a narrow gap in the package and peered into it before opening it properly.

'Why do you do that, Jess?'

'What?'

'Peep into your lunch first.'

'Used to do that at school to make sure it was something that the others wouldn't laugh at. Mum tended to give me weird lunches—cold stew, gravied dumplings, half-eaten potatoes mixed with salad—who knows what might be in there. If it looked a bit strange I'd say I wasn't hungry and throw it away without letting anyone see what was in there.'

Liam nodded. 'We were poor too; some days there wouldn't be anything to eat.'

'Oh it wasn't poverty.'

She gazed into the dancing firelight, her hands stretched towards its warmth. Above them the grey clouds thickened, cutting out even more light from the sky, making Jess's fire-dappled silhouette stand out against the blue-grey darkness. She turned towards him.

'It's funny I should end up in a religious community. When I left home I vowed never to look at another Bible, never to enter another church.'

A large drop of rain fell onto Jess's t-shirt, making a darker, spreading stain. They looked at each other and ran to the shelter of the nearest tree where they leant against its dry trunk as the rain grew from one drop to many. The rain tip-tapped on the leaves above them but luckily it didn't seem to be making its way through. Liam could smell the freshness that the rain brought as it entered the dry earth; he could feel the warmth of Jess's body as she stood next to him and he wished he could stay there forever.

He was falling in love with Jess. Sometimes as he watched her struggle to pull up a nettle, her face creased with effort and concentration, his chest filled with cotton wool and he couldn't breathe. He could have watched her child-like habit of tucking her hair behind her ears for eternity. At times the sight of a bead of sweat rolling down into the low neck of her vest top or the pinky-gold of sunburned flesh at the top of her shoulders made him so aroused that he had to turn away. But this wasn't the right time or place to fall in love. And why would someone like Jess be interested in Liam?

He was finding her nearness overpowering. He needed to think about something else, something to take his mind away from the desire he felt for her.

'What was the problem with your family?'

Jess looked towards the dying fire. 'I was an only child, born when my parents were in their early forties and both settled in their ways. My mother had longed for a child in the early years of their marriage but it hadn't happened and they both thought they would remain childless. Then I came along. They called me a gift from God but, to be honest, I arrived too late for them to make space for me in their lives.

'My father's faith was very strict and he insisted we followed their doctrine to the letter. My mother had got used to these restrictions but as I grew older they made my life a misery. I had absolutely nothing in common with my peers at school. That's one of the reasons why I worry about the children here going to school.'

'What does peers mean?'

'Sorry, Liam. Your peers are the same sort of people as you are. At school, your peers are your classmates.'

'My school friend Gaz was my peer then?'

'That's right. Now we're peers because we're both part of The Community *and* we're both doing the same work.'

Liam wanted to sit in silence holding onto the warmth that Jess's words made him feel, but he also wanted to keep Jess talking. It made him feel good that she trusted him enough to open up.

'What sort of things caused the difference between you and your peers?' His mouth felt strange shaping the new word.

'All sorts of things. At first it was because TV, music and the radio were banned in our house. My father believed that they were instruments of the devil. So I couldn't make-believe that I was a cartoon superhero, couldn't dance or sing to the latest hits, didn't know which toys I should be longing for.'

Jess looked up at the leaves overhead.

'As I grew older, my strange clothes became more noticeable. I hadn't to show any flesh so that meant long sleeves and long skirts. Trousers were definitely out of the question.'

She stroked her jeans as if to check they were there.

'My mother fought a long hard battle with my father and the school in order to find a uniform that would be acceptable to both. I made few friends and there was no one I could call a close friend.'

Jess looked up at the sky for a moment.

'It was probably for the best that I had no close friends. I couldn't have invited them home. I couldn't risk them seeing the way that my father behaved. The rules and rituals around every action. The way that he stood in the hallway and roared at my mother because of something she had done. Or not done.

'And how could I expose my cowed mother to public view? She only spoke when she was spoken to, even with me. She had long since lost the ability to make a rational decision. Her care for me was minimal to say the least. I was clean and the house was clean because cleanliness was next to godliness, but my diet was chaotic, I had no toys and the more invisible I was the better. It was expected that I would melt into the background as often as possible and I did.

'So at sixteen I rebelled. Left home, found a flat and a manual job.'

Liam smiled. 'I left home at sixteen too. Bet you made a better job of it than I did.'

'I did the best I could. I worked during the day and studied at night. I saved as much as possible and was able to go to university by the time I was twenty.

'It embarrasses me to admit that I went wild in my first year at university. Late nights, drinking, men, usual sort of thing. There suddenly seemed to be no barriers to my behaviour. I'd rejected my faith, or at least my parents' faith, I had few responsibilities and I found that the coursework came easily to me. Elijah and Paul were in the same year as me but I didn't have much to do with them at that time; they were serious dedicated students and moved in different circles to me.'

'So you've known Elijah for a long time?'

'Yes, although he was called Robert when I met him.'

'Why did he get a new name?'

'He went to America as an exchange student and was born again as a Christian. He chose the name Elijah because it means 'God is The Lord.''

Liam nodded.

Jess went on. 'Elijah came in for a fair bit of teasing when he changed his name. They nicknamed him Lige. He didn't mind at first. He laughed at the graffiti on his posters for the Bible Reading Week. It said 'Oblige Elijah, take a look at the Book.' But he didn't laugh when someone else added, 'Don't listen to them, forget the book, Lige is nothing but a fucking kook."

Jess's face became serious at the memory.

'I'd become quite friendly with Elijah by then, although I still hadn't regained my faith. I helped to take the posters down. It still upsets me when I think how much that graffiti hurt him. He became more withdrawn and was less willing to talk to me.'

Liam pulled on a piece of grass. 'What happened after university?'

'I went to Manchester and found an administration job. I really enjoyed the 'backroom' nature of the work; I liked to put my head down and 'get on with it.' I found myself a lovely little flat and settled down into a routine.

'I lost touch with Elijah and Paul for a while. But there came a time when I realised something was missing from my life. I began to look around at local churches, thinking that I needed to regain my faith. By an amazing coincidence I met Elijah in Manchester centre and he invited me to one of their prayer meetings.

'My faith blossomed in those meetings and the community spirit that Paul and Elijah developed. Eventually I moved in with them to help them with their work and I've never looked back.

'I can't believe how lucky I am that Elijah came back into my life. I'd do anything to help him and this community to do God's work.'

Jess smiled at Liam. 'So that's me. Oh look, it seems to be clearing up. We'd better get straight before Afternoon Assembly.'

# Nine

The Donnelly children have been with me about ten years now. It's almost like they're mine. Only one I have any problems with is Liam. I've been fostering for almost twenty years and I've never met a child like him. Lazy, cheeky, disobedient. I've even caught him stealing out my purse.

Still he's better than he used to be. At the beginning he wouldn't speak to me or have anything to do with me. I had to talk to him through Steven. And he called me, 'that woman.' I'd hear him talking to the twins and he'd be saying, 'What's that woman told you to do now?'

He used to encourage them to disobey me too. Said I couldn't tell them what to do because I was nothing to do with their family, I wasn't a real auntie. That's why he wouldn't call me Auntie Mary. Then, that is, he calls me Auntie Mary now, at least to my face. God knows what he calls me behind my back.

There was a point when I thought of giving up on him. Asking the Social Worker to take him into a home or something. But the Social Worker, she says to me, 'Mrs Turpin,' she says, 'Mrs Turpin, the poor boy's been through a hard time, just give it a bit longer.' So I thought about it, and I thought how upset the other three would be if Liam went away. Especially since they'd already lost their poor Mum and their Dad. Although, from what I heard, their Dad wasn't much of a loss. He's in prison now, thank God, not safe to walk the streets with bastards like him around, pardon my language.

I worry though, about how he'll turn out. He's probably going to end up like his Dad. A bad 'un. I tell him that. I say 'You'll end up in prison just like your Dad.' Then he storms out the room, slamming the door behind him. Still, you've got to tell them, haven't you, got to warn them what will happen if they don't change their ways.

So anyway, I said I'd keep Liam and he's still with me. We manage to get along most of the time. It's a struggle though, he won't get up in a morning, won't go to school, won't come home on time, won't do his homework. But I manage somehow.

No rest for the wicked I always say.

*10.30 am. Maths*

'Right you lot. Homework on my desk. Now.'

The classroom was filled with bustle, the noise of bag zips, the rustle of paper, the scraping of chairs, muttering, chattering.

'Keep it down.'

Liam stayed in his seat, head down, trying not to be noticed.

'Liam Donnelly, where's yours?'

'Kirsty was sick on it, sir.'

'Wasn't she sick on your homework last week?'

'That was Kelly, sir.'

'Do your sisters make a habit of being sick on your homework? Is there something wrong with them?'

'They've got a bug sir.'

'I'm sure they have. Have you got a note from home?'

'Auntie Mary's away and Uncle Bill can't write so I can't get a note, sir.'

'Why is it I don't believe you, Liam? This had better be the last time you don't do your homework. And just to make sure you remember I'm giving you a detention.'

'Aw, sir!'

'Detention, Donnelly.'

*

Liam and Gareth lounged against the wall waiting for Mrs Pendleton. Looking cool. Or so they hoped. Longing for the girls to look at them. Not knowing where to put themselves when they did.

'Dying for a fag.'

'Me too.'

'Do you want to skive this aft?'

'Can't. Mum's taking me to the dentist. She's coming for me at two.'

'Bollocks, fancied skiving today.'

'Tell you what, you could come to ours after school. Mum's going out.'

'Can't. Auntie Mary says I have to come straight home.' Liam crossed his eyes and put on a silly voice. 'I want you to come straight home from school, Liam. No messing about. Or else.'

He made a fist then flicked his second finger in the air.

'Stupid old cow!'

*3.30 pm Hometime*

Liam walked purposefully. In the wrong direction.

Steven ran after him, shouting. 'Liam, Liam, where you going?'

'Gaz's.'

Steven put his hand on Liam's shoulder.

'Please come home. Auntie Mary'll go spare. You'll be grounded for ever!'

Liam took Steven's hand away and looked directly into his eyes.

'So?'

# Ten

One Saturday it was raining so hard that Liam and Jess did not even try to go out into the garden to work. The children had been talking about making a Noah's Ark for ages so Liam and Jess offered to help. The first half hour was spent finding suitable materials: paper from the office; glue, scissors and crayons from the craft cupboard; aluminium foil and cereal packets from the kitchen—Liz, the Kitchen Leader, told them they couldn't use the cereal packets as they were full but Jess sneaked in when Liz wasn't looking and smuggled some out. The children were shocked but Jess told them they were communal packets so she wasn't stealing and, anyway, the cereals were in airtight packages. Later, in private, she told Liam that Liz was just a little Hitler who needed teaching a lesson.

Jonathan, age ten and full of confidence, took charge. He drew up plans and issued orders. Liam, Jess, Tammy, Louise and Gideon did as they were told and soon they were all busy colouring, cutting and sticking before giving the offcuts of paper and card to Becky who variously collected them in little piles, stuck them in her hair, hid them in her pocket, found them again, threw them in the air like confetti or carried them around in a cup she found behind the sofa. Liam suspected she also ate a few and he made sure that she wasn't given any foil or glued paper.

The group sang as they worked, and gave several versions of 'Who built the Ark?' saying that those responsible were: Jonathan, Jess, Liam, Tammy, Louise and Gideon. Their final version was 'Who didn't build the Ark?' where they pointed to Becky as the guilty party. Becky thought it was great that they were all singing her name and she kept saying 'Again, again,' until Jonathan lost his temper and told her to shut up. She cried and Jess sent Jonathan off in search of a drink and biscuit to make her smile again. It worked.

By the end of the morning they had a magnificent Ark, several human figures, any of which might have been Noah and a series of mismatched pairs of animals, many from indeterminate species or having missing limbs.

They were all very proud of their work and decided it should be on display. The six of them carefully carried the Ark and multitude of animals out to the large table in the hallway. Becky danced behind with a soggy piece of cereal packet that she said was a doggy.

Elijah peered round the door of the office. 'What's going on?'

'We've made a Noah's Ark, 'Lijah,' said Tammy

'Very apt,' Elijah said.

'Apt?' asked Liam.

'Yes. It's just right to put these little monkeys in.'

Elijah tickled Tammy and Louise to make them giggle.

As the group marched back to the Social Room to clean up, the children sang:

Who built the Ark?
Brother 'Lijah built the Ark.


After lunch, Jess and Liam asked Will, that day's Leader, where they could help most. He suggested the kitchen. Liz had discovered the loss of the cereal packets and turned them away at first. It took several apologies before she relented and allowed them in. She set Jess peeling potatoes and Liam chopping onions. Jim, who'd also been forced indoors by the weather, was washing up. They chatted as they worked.

Liam asked Jim what had brought him to The Larches.

Jim smiled and said, 'It was the drugs, man,' refusing to be drawn any further.

'What about you Liz? How did you get here from Bonnie Scotland?'

Liz was busy making rhubarb pie—she was less of an ogre when she was cooking.

'I left Scotland when I was seventeen. Ran away from home because of a holiday romance. You know what it's like.'

Liam nodded.

'Got married to Terry and Jason was born almost straight away. I got a job in the hospital kitchen and we were doing okay.'

She paused, leaning against the worktop and gazing off into the distance. Then she picked up the flour and shook it vigorously.

'Then, when Jason was eighteen, he collapsed in the street suddenly. I was at work so I was soon at his bedside. An aneurysm had ruptured, causing a brain haemorrhage; there was nothing anyone could do so I just sat by his bedside all night, talking to him and holding his hand as he got colder and colder.'

Another cloud of flour rose into the air.

'When he died I couldn't bear it. Couldn't leave the house, didn't even want to leave my bed, I wouldn't talk to anyone, not even Terry. It killed what little there was between us and eventually Terry left.'

Liz lifted the rolling pin in the air and banged it down on the pastry.

'One day I seemed to have a little more energy and went into town. To buy tablets. Big bottles of Paracetamol from every chemist I knew so they wouldn't get suspicious. Then suddenly I felt really tired and sat on the steps of the bandstand looking down at the floor.

Everything seemed so hopeless: I didn't even have enough energy to go home and take that final step.

'Rachel was giving out pamphlets with Paul nearby. She came over to ask if I was alright. I said, "I can't go on." She seemed to understand straightaway and they brought me back here.'

Liam suddenly thought about his own journey to The Larches in Paul's car. He couldn't remember much apart from making some comments about Paul's hair.

'Those first few weeks are still all mixed up in my mind. They fed me and told me what to do, when to work, when to sleep. I had people to talk to, people who didn't run away or change the subject when I mentioned Jason. They prayed with me and for me.'

Liz looked out of the window.

'One day, I noticed the sun was shining. Life got gradually better from that moment. I'm here because I needed help and this community gave it to me. That was five years ago and now it's my whole life. Thank God.'

Liam patted Liz's flour-arm with his onion-hand. She brushed him away with a 'Get off me, you big softy,' but she was smiling as she said it.

Dinner that night was doubly good because Liam had played a part in making the Shepherd's Pie. He sat with Rebecca and fed Becky her rhubarb pie and custard. What a mess. Then Becky wanted to feed him. She put a large blob of custard on his nose before trying to lick it off. He blamed the tears in his eyes on laughing too hard.

Rebecca had to help in the kitchen after dinner so Jess and Liam agreed to take Becky to Circle Time with them. As they walked, they each held her hand and swung her into the air.

They began with a discussion in groups and then Paul asked them to make two larger groups for a game. Jess and Liam's Group joined together and they sat down in their circle, keeping Becky between them.

Paul said 'We're going to do the Thankful game tonight. Tell you what, let's make it more difficult—we'll do an Alphabet Thankful. Some of you will have to go twice.' He laughed, 'And you'll be the lucky ones who get XYZ as well!'

Tom: I'm thankful for ... Clap, clap, Alphabet Thankful Game
   Pat: Clap, clap, Bible
   Rachel: Clap, clap, Circle Time
   Josh: Clap, clap, Disciples
   Gideon: Clap, clap, Extra Helpings
   Andrea: Clap, clap, Friends
   Fred: Clap, clap, Good Friends
   Ruth: Clap, clap, Happiness
   Jim: Clap, clap, Ideals
   Will: Clap, clap, Joyfulness
   Liam: Clap, clap, Kindness
Becky: Clappity, clap, clap. She looked at Jess. Jess whispered in her ear. Becky shouted 'Lijah' and grinned round at the rest of the circle.
   Jess: Clap, clap, Morning Meeting
   Gemma: Clap, clap, 'Nowing Everyone
   Mary: Clap, clap, Obedience
   Ian: Clap, clap, Parables
   Mel: Clap, clap, Quoting the Bible
   George: Clap, clap, Reading the Bible
   Cynthia: Clap, clap, Social Hour
   Ray: Clap, clap, Taking Responsibility
   Tom: Clap, clap, Understanding more about God
   Pat: Clap, clap, Very Good Cooking
   Rachel: Clap, clap, Working for God
   Josh: Clap, clap, Xamining the Bible
   Gideon: Clap, clap, You

The circle let go of the laughter which had been bubbling up inside them. Paul let them calm down before he said, 'I think there was a bit of cheating going on in there, don't you?

'Right, we'll do the Ball Game before we make our Big Circle. We'll be using last week's routine so I hope you can all remember it. Becky, sweetheart, come and stand with me so you don't get hurt.'

Becky looked at Liam. He took her hand and walked her to Paul before rejoining his circle.

*Social Hour*

Liam sat, feeling cosy and contented, in his favourite chair in his favourite corner near the fire. His legs were warm from the fire and Methuselah the cat was on his knee, purring as Liam absentmindedly stroked him. He could see what was happening in the two joined rooms but he didn't need to take part in any of it if he didn't want to.

The crackling of the fire merged with the background hubbub as he listened to Jess talking to Elijah and George. She was talking about the children being homeschooled as she worried about them not fitting in at their schools. That morning, Tammy had told her she had been teased at school because she didn't know when Coronation Street was on. It was an old topic of conversation, with strong feelings on either side; Jess drawing on her personal experience whilst Elijah felt it was good for Community children to be in school because they could pass on the word. Jess had told Liam that she hoped the story of Tammy's upset would persuade Elijah to think seriously about homeschooling.

Methuselah suddenly dug his claws into Liam's knee. Liam jumped and then lifted Methuselah up and dropped him on the floor, careful to avoid any more contact between claw and skin. 'Naughty cat,' he scolded in such a gentle voice that no cat would ever know they were in trouble. When he looked up again, Jess and Elijah were leaving the room.

Suddenly there was some amicable shouting over in the Dining Room half. They were arguing about a word in Scrabble and Gideon was sent to the library to find the dictionary. When he returned, Will looked through the dictionary and punched the air in victory.

Rebecca arrived carrying a bathed and pyjama'd Becky. As soon as she put the child on the floor Becky headed for Liam. She gave him a kiss and stroked Methuselah who had climbed back onto Liam's knee. The book that Jonathan had made her in the afternoon was on the arm of Liam's chair and she took it to show Rebecca. They looked at the book together.

'Fish.' Becky blew out her cheeks and opened and closed her mouth to impersonate a fish. Then she turned the page.

'Thusalah.' Becky pointed to the cat on Liam's knee. Liam picked up a paw and waved it at her. Becky smiled. Methuselah snatched his paw away.

Rebecca turned the page. Becky pointed. 'Doggy.'

'What does doggy say?' Rebecca asked.

'Woof. Woof.'

Becky turned the page. 'Jesus.' She put her hands together as if in prayer and closed her eyes for a moment. Then she opened her eyes, turned to her mother and wriggled in excitement. She had a new sentence to show off. 'Jesus loves me.'

And me, thought Liam. And me.

# Eleven

Liam and Auntie Mary are having another big row. I hate it when they argue like that; I have to come out of the room. Kelly and Steven don't leave—Kelly just thinks it's funny and Steven takes Auntie Mary's side.

They're arguing about what Liam's going to do after his exams. Auntie Mary says if Liam's not going to stay on at school he has to get a job. Uncle Bill's arranged an interview for him at his friend's shop. Liam says he's not going to sell poxy pants to poxy pensioners.

I can hear them shouting. Liam keeps saying that he's going to run away. Auntie Mary says she's not going to let him show her up with the Social Worker by doing that.

I hope he doesn't go. I'd really miss him. Who would I talk to? Kelly gets on my nerves. Always has to be better than me! And Steven's such a bloody goody-goody. Liam's the only one who understands me.

Liam slammed his bedroom door and flung himself on the bed. He could feel his heart pounding in his chest and his breath was heavy in his mouth. Just at that moment he hated everything and everybody. He couldn't stand it in that place much longer; they didn't understand: they didn't even seem to like him.

He thought about how he could escape. It was too risky to leave straightaway—they'd be watching him. Better to behave for a few days. Make them relax; think he'd learnt his lesson. He'd go for the interview and be polite. And take the Maths exam the following Thursday, then Friday he'd leave the house as if he was going to take Geography. But he wouldn't go to school, he'd go straight to the station and catch the next train; it would be late afternoon before they realised he was gone and by that time he'd be well on his way.

Money was a problem though. He had twenty pounds in his Post Office Savings account. Auntie Mary thought she'd hidden the book but he knew all her hiding places. But that was nowhere near enough.

He searched his mind for other sources of money. Steven had a moneybox on his bedside cabinet. It probably had about five pounds in it. He had no qualms about taking that—Steven meant nothing to him. He was also fairly certain he could persuade Kirsty to 'lend' him a fiver—she was usually a soft touch. It was no good asking Kelly; she was so tight she'd never lend him anything. Said he never paid her back; which was true but she didn't need to draw attention to it.

Thirty quid. He'd need more than that. No chance trying for Auntie Mary's purse, she'd learnt her lesson and kept it locked away. If he could stay awake the night before he'd try and sneak into their bedroom and empty Uncle Bill's wallet. With a bit of luck he wouldn't notice before Liam left. Plus he was sure he could nick some stuff from the shop to sell to his mates.

He smiled to himself. It was going to be alright.

# Twelve

When the kitchen extension was completed everyone was given a day off to celebrate. This didn't mean it would be a sleep-late, feet-up kind of day. The house was even busier than normal getting ready for the blessing of the extension at six pm followed by a big party at seven. There was lots of work to be done.

Liam had agreed to help with the decorations and had blown up quite a few balloons when Rebecca told him she wanted a banner to write 'Lord Bless Our Extension,' on.

'Bet Jess knows where one is; I'll go and find her.'

Rebecca thanked him and went off to talk Becky out of pulling down the streamers someone had wrapped round the new fridge.

Liam went to the Leader's office first. It was empty. He wandered round the building and then decided to look upstairs. Maybe they were in the back office. When that was empty, he turned to go back downstairs but heard a noise from a nearby bedroom. The door was slightly ajar. He went to open it fully but then stopped: he could see a mirror on the wall reflecting an image of Elijah and Jess. Elijah was seated and Jess stood at his side, her hand on his shoulder. As he watched, Elijah rested his head against her breasts and she bent over and kissed the top of his head. Liam stopped breathing for a moment; he watched as Jess lifted her hand from Elijah's shoulder and gently pushed his head away.

He raised his hand to knock at the door. But then he froze. He saw Jess kneel down in front of Elijah. She looked up into Elijah's face. Elijah smiled down at her. Her hands moved towards his waist and slowly, slowly began to undo his belt.

No, it can't be. Don't do that, Jess. Don't do that. Not with him, not with Elijah. How could she do that? No Jess. Not now. Not here. Can't see, can't breathe. Jess and Dad. No. Mum and Elijah. No, no, no! Jess and Elijah. What's that roaring? What's that noise? It's all dark, dark, scary, dark. Mum. What's Mum doing? Jess, please don't, don't do that. Mum, don't do that. Who was it? Was it Mum? Was it Jess? Can't be Mum, she's dead. Don't, don't, Dad, don't. Just blackness, so scared, so afraid. Where is everyone? Where can I go? What can I do? Who was it? It was Jess, Jess and Elijah. Have to get away from them, from that. How can they be doing that? How can … Jess … do … that … with … him?

When the pictures in his mind began to flicker, when he could see through them, he found himself at the old barn. His breathing was irregular, his heart seemed to be out of control and he hurt all over. He looked around him. The sun was shining but everything was dark. He couldn't see properly. He sat for about an hour, he didn't know what else to do.

Then he heard a noise. Instinct made him hide amongst the trees and he watched as a truck arrived with its load covered by a tarpaulin. The driver and Paul climbed down from the cab and began to unload the contents.

He heard the two men talking inside the barn. This was his chance. He climbed into the back of the truck and covered himself with the tarpaulin. Paul and the driver came out of the barn, still talking. The driver climbed into the cab, slammed the door and started the engine.

It was hot and breathless as the truck bumped and swerved along country roads. Eventually it stopped and Liam heard the driver get out.

He left it a couple of moments and then peered out. He didn't know which town it was but he knew he was in a pub car park. The driver was nowhere in sight so he climbed out of the truck and ran out into the street.

He walked towards the centre of town and, when he saw a burger bar he headed towards it.

When he opened the door the artificial light almost blinded him and as he approached the counter he noticed that all the staff had clown-like smiles pasted on their spotty unhealthy faces. He ordered a burger and a large Coke. He wasn't hungry, just doing what people do in those places.

He sat near the window. Outside two cars had a near miss and Liam watched as their drivers wound down their windows to swear and shake their fists at each other. Turning away, he saw a little girl about Becky's age in a high chair at the next table. Her family ignored her unclear words 'Fies,' 'Burga,' and they didn't follow her chubby pointed finger to see what she was looking at. When she reached over to pull her mother's sleeve to get her attention, her mother slapped the tiny hand away.

'Sit still and be quiet.'

The burger tasted like the polystyrene container it had come in. The Coke fizzed in his mouth and made his stomach feel bloated. He looked around the room again. The staff still smiled their artificial smiles but the customers didn't smile at all. Mothers, fathers, brothers, sisters argued with each other. The background noise was horrendous. He'd chosen the wrong place. There was a pub across the road. He could hide from himself in there so he left the burger place with a sigh of relief.

He narrowly avoided being hit by a car as he crossed the road. He was no longer used to traffic. As he entered

The White Lion, a dirty unshaven man stumbled into him and said, 'Get out my bloody way!' Liam, off balance, staggered into the darkness of the pub and caught hold of the only thing he could see, a brightly lit slot machine that clattered and clanged. The man feeding coin after coin into the machine glared at him for interrupting his game.

Gradually his eyes adjusted to the light. People huddled over small tables—mainly men, mostly on their own. The bar shone brightly at the far end of the room, the fluorescent lighting bleaching the faces of the staff leaving them ghost-like. Progress was slow as he walked towards the bar; his feet stuck to the carpet at each step.

And then the smell hit his memory buds. It brought up the sour flavour of his Dad coming home shouting from the pub; incapable of normal speech by lunchtime or lying unconscious in the street as the sun went down. The polystyrene burger appeared at the back of his throat, pushed up by the fizz of the Coke. He turned and staggered out in much the same manner as he had entered, only this time the propulsion was his own need to find fresh air.

Once outside he found a wall to lean against and watched the battle as pedestrians tried to cross the road and the cars ignored them. He observed people struggling down the street laden with heavy bags of inessentials. He saw their faces show every negative emotion: distress, pain, anger, frustration. He remembered feeling like that.

He needed somewhere to think; to sort it all out and make decisions. He needed to talk to God. Where could he go? The first two churches were locked and he had to search the streets until he found one with an unlocked door.

Inside the church the lofty air was cool. In some places the sun made its way through the coloured glass and a row of lit votive candles flickered in the shadow by the wall. But they didn't add any warmth, merely highlighted the sluggish dust motes that lumbered through the air.

When he chose a pew and sat down the seat was hard, the wood made firm by years of polish and varnish. It had no give, just slither and slide. Pulling out the kneeler he slipped down on to it and tipped his head back, looking for God in this place of worship. But God wasn't there. Not for Liam. His God was in the fresh air, in the wind rushing through the trees, touching his face with warmth from the sun, cooling his skin with the rain. His God made green plants push their way through the earth into life. Liam's God couldn't make his way through those thick stone walls.

In this place he was truly alone. And he wept. He wept for the young Liam who'd seen and felt things no child should. He wept for the adult Liam who'd had to look at life through an alcoholic haze in order to survive. He wept for the idyllic life at The Larches which seemed to have suddenly taken on a nightmare quality.

Eventually the tears dried. His mind was empty; it had drained itself dry. He sat in silence. Then the prayer came:

God grant us the serenity to accept the things we cannot change, the courage to change the things we can, and the wisdom to know the difference.

Things he couldn't change. He couldn't change what he had seen. Jess and Elijah. Couldn't rub it out and make it disappear. He wouldn't be able to make Jess love him however much he wanted it.

The courage to change the things he could. What could he change? He could change his romantic dreams to fit with practical reality. He could stop running away from unpleasant experiences. He could leave this God-forsaken town and return to The Larches where at least life offered him some hope.

The wisdom to know the difference. No one knew as yet that he'd left The Larches. If he could accept what he'd seen between Jess and Elijah he could go back.

And he knew he wanted to go home. To The Larches. To his new family and Jess. The real one not the romantic dream. The decision was made. Go back. See what happens. The door slammed shut behind him when he left the church, but he didn't notice.

He found a taxi to take him back and asked the driver to drop him on the main road. Tom was on duty at the gatehouse. 'Where you bin, then?' he said with a grin,

'Secret mission for Elijah.'

'In your dreams, mate, in your dreams!'

Liam laughed. 'You're just jealous.'

As he walked up the drive the house glowed golden in the late afternoon sun. Little Becky was playing with the other children on the lawn as her mother watched from the steps. When Becky saw him she shouted 'Liam, Liam' and ran as fast as she was able towards him. He picked her up and swung her round a couple of times as she squealed with joy, then he balanced her on his hip and carried her toward her mother. When they got to the steps he put Becky down and sat beside Rebecca.

'Isn't this the most perfect place in the world?' she asked.

He looked around. The sun was low in the sky, tingeing some of the clouds with pink. Children laughed and ran on the smooth green lawn which stretched down towards the ancient trees bordering the property. Hanging baskets shared their perfume with the breeze. Behind him there were family noises, chatting, shrieks of laughter. Not perfect but the best place he'd ever lived in.

'What better place to bring up a child?' Rebecca asked. Liam felt something at his knee. It was Becky with a bent and battered daisy clutched in her sticky hand. She handed it to him solemnly.

'Fower.'

He looked down at her and echoed her solemnity. 'Thank you, sweetheart.'

Rebecca was just saying, 'I hope I can stay here for the rest of my life,' when Will appeared at the top of the steps.

'Come on, guys, the blessing's about to start and then it's party time!'

# Thirteen

'My name's Liam and I'm an alcoholic.

'I started drinking at fourteen. I used to steal money from my foster mother's purse to pay for it. When she found out and locked her purse away from me, I stole from local shops.

'At sixteen I ran away from home and went to London. Spent a couple of years on the streets, scavenging to keep myself in drink. I was willing to do anything just to find enough money for a bottle of vodka. Anything!

'I came back up north when I was nineteen. Shared a caravan with some bloke in Manchester for a while. It was hard. I struggled to find a job, no qualifications, no references, you know what it's like.

'And when I found a job I couldn't keep it. I got drunk or I couldn't be bothered or I helped myself to money that someone had left lying around. Or not left lying around. Twenty jobs in six months. Word got round and then no one at all would employ me. Couldn't pay the rent on the caravan. So there I was; back on the streets.

'Then I woke up one morning and found myself covered in blood. It wasn't mine. I didn't have a mark on me. To this day I don't know where it came from…'

# Fourteen

*Assembly Room, several weeks later*

Everyone was present. George stood facing the room. Elijah sat on the front row with Gemma, Liam, Pat, Ruth and Tom.

George began to speak. 'This is a very special Afternoon Assembly. Today we have five people signing their commitment forms. That will bring us to a total of forty-eight full members. This week we've also welcomed two new members and there are probably another three coming next week. This is a very important time in our history.

'I'm proud to say that I was one of the first members. Sometimes, when I remember the prayer meetings in the front room of a terraced house in Manchester, I look around at the wonderful house we now have and smile. How lucky we are to live somewhere like this.'

He looked up at the stain on the ceiling caused by last week's leak. 'Still needs a bit of work though!'

His laugh was echoed around the room.

'But we don't mind work here at The Larches, do we? We're happy to work long hard hours doing the Lord's work.

'I used to work long hard hours before I joined but it was a different sort of work. The sort of work that fills your mind but doesn't touch your heart, that puts bread on the table but doesn't nourish your soul. I had my own business. I called it successful. Profits went up year by year and so did my bank balance. I thought I was doing well but, in truth, I had a bank account full of money and a life full of nothing. My wife had left, taking the children because I couldn't, wouldn't find time for them. I was too busy looking for the right deal, the one that would make me rich, make me enough money to… well, I didn't know to what because there was never enough money, no matter how much my bank balance was.'

He paused.

'Then one day I met Elijah. I was rushing from a meeting back to the office and I literally bumped into him. Knocked him and his leaflets flying. God wanted to make sure I didn't miss him.

'Suddenly I no longer felt the urge to rush back. We went for coffee and I called my secretary to say I'd be late. In fact I didn't return to work that day. I spent it with Elijah. And God. That was when God came into my heart. He made me look at my life with clear eyes and I knew, I knew, that my money and business were worthless without him. Before long I had freed myself of my business.

'The day I signed my commitment papers I felt as free as it is possible to feel. I knew I could fly because God had given me wings.'

He looked at the front row.

'And now today these five will take that step. Set themselves free of the mundane obligations of the worldly life so they can live their lives giving the Glory to God.'

'I'd like to end on a reading from Corinthians and then we'll witness the signing of the commitment forms.

"So if anyone is in Christ, there is a new creation: everything old has passed away; see, everything has become new! [18]All this is from God, who reconciled us to himself through Christ, and has given us the ministry of reconciliation". Two Corinthians five, verses seventeen to eighteen.'

Elijah walked to the front and stood next to George. He held five official documents which he placed on the table in front of him. He took a gold fountain pen from his shirt pocket and placed it next to the documents.

'Gemma, can you come to the front.'

Gemma walked slowly to the front and stood between Elijah and George. Elijah uncapped the pen, handed it to her then pointed to the place for her to sign. She bent forward and signed. Elijah took the pen from her, signed his name then gave it to George. George signed, put the cap back on the pen and replaced the pen on the table. He nodded to Gemma and she knelt. George and Elijah each placed a hand on her shoulder. Elijah was the one who spoke and, at the end of each line, the congregation whispered, 'Yes, Lord.';

'Lord, let us welcome our sister to our community,

'Let her be a part of us and us a part of her.

'Let us all feel stronger for having this new member,

'Let us all rejoice in His presence.'

It was Liam next. He had been waiting for that day and, although he had been nervous earlier, now he felt happy and confident.

The previous six weeks had been difficult. When he had seen Jess at the blessing, he'd dropped a plate and she'd insisted on helping him pick up the pieces. His hands were shaking because she was near and he cut his finger. It was agony for him as she insisted on cleaning up the cut and putting on a plaster for him. But they'd worked side by side since then and gradually the pain had eased

He still loved Jess. She was in a special place in his heart, a place so deep within him that he knew nothing could ever change those feelings. And he would stay here in the community for ever just to be near to her.

But it wasn't just his love for Jess that made him want to make this commitment. He'd realised that he had a chance here, a chance to make a good life for himself, one where he was surrounded by the friends who made up his new family. It was a place where he could leave his unhappy past behind him and grow into a stronger happier person, secure in his love for God and God's love for him.

'Liam.'

He strode forward and took his place between Elijah and George. He looked at his Commitment Form:

I, Liam Joseph Donnelly, hereby commit my life to The Community at The Larches, hereinafter referred to as The Community.

I agree that I will:
- Remain within The Community for the rest of my natural life
- Obey the word of God at all times
- Accept the authority of Elijah as Head of The Community
- Put The Community's needs before my personal needs
- Live within the boundaries which have been communally established
- Relinquish all links with friends and family from my previous life.
- Sign over all financial assets to communal funds.

I confirm that I have:
- Discussed any outstanding financial obligations with The Community's solicitors
- Made sufficient provision for such obligations so that there can be no claim on The Community's assets.
- Informed all relevant people and organisations that I am no longer to be contacted in relation to anything involving the secular world.

Signed: ..................LIAM JOSEPH DONNELLY

Witness: ..................ELIJAH ROBERT ELLIS

Witness: ..................GEORGE JAMIESON


My name's Liam
I've all I need here
Up at The Larches
Up at The Larches

All my family
Here to support me
Up at The Larches
Up at The Larches

This is where
God wants me to be
Up at The Larches
Up at The Larches.

II

# Fifteen

As I turned into the drive I could see Jess and the children on the lawn in front of the house. She'd got her wish and had been running the homeschool for nearly two years. Every subject was based on the Bible. She got most of her teaching materials from a Christian organisation in America, but she adapted quite a lot of it. She didn't like the way that the children were expected to sit still all the time and not interact with each other. Elijah had had some input too because he didn't always agree with their interpretation of the Bible. The only one who studied different things was Jonathan as he was doing the GCSE syllabus; as would Gideon the following year.

The children had blossomed during that time; Jess worked hard to make sure that they kept up their work and she added extra topics to keep them interested. We all helped, even me. I taught the children about plants and flowers—their names and how they grow.

I parked the van and climbed out as Tammy came running over to me.

'Liam, Liam, we've been meeting trees. Do you want to have a go?'

I was confused. How could you meet a tree? I looked over Tammy's head at Jess.

'Come on. Liam. It'll be fun.'

I'd told Ian I'd come and help him dig over the new field after the deliveries, but that could wait a while. Gideon waved a scarf in the air shouting, 'You've got to be blindfolded.' He tried to reach up to put it on, but I had to kneel down so he could reach. He fastened it so tightly over my eyes, nose and mouth that not only could I not see, I couldn't breathe either. 'Bit enthusiastic there,

Gideon,' I said as I loosened the scarf. Then I heard Tammy's voice.

'Stand up. That's it. Now take my hand.'

Her warm fingers took hold of mine and she pulled me along behind her.

'Slow down, slow down. I can't see where I'm going, remember.'

Jess took my other hand. Her fingers were cool and made mine tingle; as did her voice when she said, 'I won't let you fall.'

They led me round in circles for ages. Then we stopped and Tammy explained what I had to do.

'This is your tree. You've got to get to know it. Learn all about its bark and bumps and lumps and branches.'

I put out a finger and touched the rough bark and then I used my whole hand to stroke it.

Daniel watched my hand moving and whispered, 'That's what I did.' He'd been with us about six weeks and he was finding it hard to settle in. It didn't help that he and his father had to share a room with me, Tom, Ian and Josh. He seemed to feel overwhelmed by it all.

Louise said, 'Put your arms right round it and hug it. That's what I did.'

I stretched my arms round its trunk. It must have been very thick because I could only just reach. I could feel a rough patch at the other side, probably a scar. I moved my hands upwards and found where the branches were; there were two I could reach quite easily and then another four that I could just touch.

Jess asked, 'Do you know your tree now? Would you be able to recognise it again?'

I nodded, although I wasn't certain. Tammy took one hand, Jess took the other and we walked round in circles again till I felt dizzy. When we stopped, Louise pulled me to my knees so she could take the blindfold off. As I blinked at the light, Jess and the children began shouting.

'Which is your tree?'

'Which one?'

'You've got to find your tree now.'

I looked around. There were a lot of trees but most of them were too thin to be mine or they didn't have enough branches. I narrowed it down to two.

'Can I go and have a closer look?'

'Is that cheating, Jess?' Gideon liked to play by the rules.

'No, it's not cheating.'

I walked around the two possible trees. They were both oaks. One had its branches in the right place. 'I think it's this one.' Then I saw the scar. 'Yes, it's definitely this one.'

They all clapped and cheered.

'That was my tree as well,' said Louise.

'We all got ours right too,' said Tammy.

Jess clapped her hands and said, 'Okay, it's break time. Go and ask Liz for your drinks and I'll meet you in the Library at half past. Don't be late.'

The children raced off. Jess and I followed; I needed to check the post and Jess wanted to talk to Elijah. It was cool inside the house. Jess disappeared into the office while I searched through the envelopes lying on the hall table. I was expecting a seed catalogue. It wasn't there but there was a letter about an order I'd made from another company. As I read it I heard Rebecca's voice.

'Liam, can we have a word with you.'

I turned. Rebecca was coming out of the Social Room, pulling a tearful Becky behind her. Becky was now four or very nearly five as she kept telling me.

'Right Becky, tell Liam what you did.'

Becky peered out from behind her mother. 'I stole a flower from the big greenhouse for my dolly. She likes flowers.'

I knelt on the floor so I was on her eye-level.

'The flowers in the greenhouse are for us to sell so we have pennies to pay for things. We can't afford to lose any of the selling ones. If you ask me for a flower I can always find you one from the not-selling ones. Did you remember to close the greenhouse door?'

Becky nodded. She'd learnt that lesson very early on.

'I'm sorry, Liam. It was Jesus's fault though, he told me to do it.'

I kept my smile hidden as Rebecca pulled on Becky's hand to turn her so they were facing each other.

'I'm really cross now. I've told you not to use Jesus as an excuse when you do naughty things. For punishment I'm not going to let you do drawing in Jess's school this afternoon. You can sit with me whilst I do the mending instead.'

'I like Jess's school.' Becky's lip trembled and her voice rose. 'Please let me go.'

'Don't argue or I won't let you go tomorrow either. Come on now; let's see if Liz needs anything doing.'

The two of them went off towards the kitchen.

I remembered I needed to pick up some more cards from the office. They were for customers to use when they gave someone our flowers. It had been Jonathan's idea. There was a little picture of a garden on the front and space to write, with 'Eden's Garden,' and our telephone number on the back. Jonathan printed them off on the computer, but he was going to show me how to do it myself. I was gradually learning how to do all sorts of things on the computer—Paul had taught me how to do the gardening business accounts in a special program he'd set up for me.

I went into the office and found the cards. Jess and Elijah were in the back room; I could hear their voices. I thought about that day when I'd seen her with Elijah. It hadn't affected the love I felt for her; I didn't know why. Maybe it was just that she was such a special person; she always made me feel good about myself. I'd never told her how I felt. I'd kept it deep inside me because I knew that she was too good for me in every way possible. I couldn't risk letting her know how I felt; I just didn't have the confidence. Instead I held her safe in my heart and I was happy to live in a house where I could see her every day.

Of course I knew she wasn't perfect. She had faults. Sometimes she got angry or she went against the rules if they didn't suit her. You should have heard her going on about the new rules on women not wearing jeans and keeping themselves covered up. But she cared about everyone in that Community, going out of her way to make sure that everyone was happy and she always listened to what they had to say.

And anyway I was no saint. There were things in my past that I was very ashamed of and there were times in The Community when my faith let me down. Jess understood. She knew that, however much I tried to live my life according to God's wishes, sometimes I became selfish or I didn't understand what He wanted me to do. When that happened, Jess listened to me and talked it through.

I still hadn't fully got over my dislike of Elijah either, even though I knew the things he did and said were in The Community's best interests. I didn't always understand what made him make the decisions he made and there were times when I felt angry inside about it. But even then I accepted that he cared about all of us and his actions were according to God's will.

Another thing I still didn't understand was about couples in The Community. I'd watched everyone and, as far as I knew, there were no couples there. I'd known right from the beginning that they weren't admitted but what would happen if two Community members decided they wanted to be a couple? Would they have to leave?

Or would it be alright if they were already used to putting The Community and God first? Would Elijah allow that?

I used to have this dream sometimes. In the dream I'd go to Jess and tell her I loved her. She was always sitting under an apple tree, her hair shining in the sun. Everything was all soft, like in those films where they do something with the focus. She'd look up into my face and say that she loved me too. She'd put out both hands and I'd take hold of them and help her to stand, then we'd float off towards the house and into the office to see Elijah.

This was where the dream would become a nightmare. We'd both speak at the same time, telling him, 'We love each other.' He'd let out a great roar and he'd grow and grow till he filled the whole room, pushing me and Jess apart. Then the room would start to crack and break up and suddenly I'd be standing alone in the ruins of the house, everyone gone, leaving me all alone. I'd wake up sweating and shaking, knowing that I should never tell Jess how I felt—I could only carry on day to day, enjoying the time I got to spend with her.

I took the cards outside and left them in the van ready for when the shopkeepers asked for them. The business was doing really well. When we started we hadn't been sure whether to invest some money from the catering business to give us a head start or whether we should start really small. We decided to risk it and bought two greenhouses and it paid off.

We mainly sold flowers, like Elijah said right at the beginning, but we also sold houseplants and some vegetables from the kitchen garden. Our customers were local newsagents, service stations and small shops. They liked us because they didn't have to buy big amounts and we picked up any surplus the following day. There usually wasn't much left over because our quality was so good and, as time had gone on, we'd worked out between us what was likely to go and how much they needed.

When I got out to the field I found that Ian had made a good start. He was my full time helper. I also got quite a bit of help from the others. It was good running a business in a community because there were always extra people to help at busy times. Jonathan helped me a lot too, when he wasn't doing his schoolwork. He planned to work with me full time after his exams.

I took off my jacket, grabbed a spade and began to work alongside Ian.

# Sixteen

It was a Tuesday morning and as usual I got up about five. The others didn't like to be woken before seven thirty so I dressed quietly and went out to the gardens to make up the flowers for the day.

Then I went in to breakfast. It was good to be on the early sitting; there weren't many people there so there wasn't the usual clatter and chaos. I looked round for Ian but he wasn't there. He must have overslept so I couldn't tell him what I wanted him to do that day. I went out into the hallway and wrote him a note and pinned it to the bulletin board, then I went back and piled my plate high.

When I'd nearly finished, Jonathan appeared. I was surprised to see him at that time; he had a reputation as a late riser—Rachel got really angry with him sometimes.

'You're early this morning.'

'I wondered if I could come out with you on your rounds.'

'What about your schoolwork? I don't want to be in trouble with Jess.'

'It was her idea. She's making biscuits with the younger ones this morning. She said it would be better experience for me to come out delivering with you instead of being there in all that chaos. I was supposed to ask last night but I forgot.'

'That's fine but I'm about to go. What about your breakfast?'

'I'll just take a piece of toast. I'm not really hungry.'

'Okay, but I don't want you moaning about being starving.'

'I won't. Honest.'

Jonathan buttered and jammed a piece of toast and followed me out to the van. He helped to load up, using one hand until he'd finished eating. I couldn't concentrate on what I was doing because I was so worried he'd make the wrappings sticky.

'Right, Jonathan. Mr Kumar's our last customer. We've made good time. Thanks for your help.'

'Liam, I'm hungry.'

'What did I say? I knew a piece of toast wasn't enough for a growing lad like you.'

'Can we get something to eat?'

'I suppose I could get you a bar of chocolate from Mr Kumar's.'

'No, some proper breakfast! I'm absolutely starving.'

'Can't it wait till we get back?'

'No. Please, please, please.'

'Oh, alright, there's a café just down the road. I'll pay for it out of my float money but remind me to get a receipt. I'll have to sort it out with George when we get back.'

In the café it took ages for Jonathan to decide what he wanted; he wasn't used to menus, but he was determined to make the best of this strange experience. In the end he chose something called 'Superbreakfast,' which claimed to have 'at least two of everything a breakfast usually has plus more.' I had a toasted teacake and a coffee.

It was weird sitting in a place like that, eating with a lot of strangers. It was a long time since I'd done that and I thought back to that day when I'd done a runner. I remembered how I'd looked around thinking how unreal it all seemed and that everyone looked so unhappy. The people around us didn't seem that bad, but they still didn't look as happy as the people I was used to seeing at home.

Then I noticed someone who looked like Auntie Mary and, when I looked harder, I realised it *was* Auntie Mary.

When she turned in my direction I put my hand up to cover my face and hoped she hadn't seen me. Taking a ten pound note from my pocket I pushed it towards Jonathan and said, 'I've just remembered something I have to do. It'll take about ten minutes. When you've finished, pay the woman behind the counter with that. I'll meet you back at the van. Will you be okay?'

He looked confused but nodded. I pushed my way out of the café and rushed away, dodging round corners and up back streets so that I was sure she wasn't following me. Then I leant against a cold brick wall to try to calm down. My breathing was uneven and my legs were shaking.

It had been a lifetime since I'd seen her. About fifteen years. She was a part of my old life, the one I'd put behind me when I joined the community. The old Liam hadn't liked her, had hated her in fact. I didn't hate her anymore; I didn't hate anyone. I'd realised that she'd tried her best with me, but that didn't mean I wanted any contact. And anyway, when I'd committed my life to The Community, I'd promised to, what was it, relinquish all links with my previous life so I couldn't speak to her, even if I wanted to.

I took several deep breaths and consciously relaxed my body. I was fairly sure she hadn't recognised me and, even if she had, the odds were she wouldn't want anything to do with me. I'd hurt her enough in the past, why would she want to see me now? Still, I took a back route to the van; just to be sure I didn't meet up with her. Jonathan was waiting for me. As I walked towards him he waved a piece of paper at me.

'I remembered to get a receipt.'

'That's good. Now get in, we have to go.'

When I'd started the van he asked, in a puzzled voice, 'Where did you go?'

'When?'

'When you left the café?'

'Oh I just popped back to have a word with Mr Kumar about tomorrow's order, that's all. It's someone's birthday so he wants a special bouquet.'

'Can I help make it?'

'What?'

'The bouquet.'

'We'll see, Jonathan, we'll see.'

He slouched down in his seat and looked at the floor. 'I'll take that as a no then. It's not fair, everyone treats me like a kid and I'm not!'

'Okay, I can't let you help with this one but I promise I'll let you help with the next one.'

He lifted his head and stared out of the window for a while. Then he turned towards me and patted his stomach.

'That breakfast was good. Do you think we could do this again?'

'I don't think so. Once is quite enough.'

# Seventeen

It was a week or so later and the Dining Room and Morning Room were being decorated. It was absolute chaos, furniture all over the place. The Assembly Room was full and there was other stuff piled up in the hallway and corridors. It was a good job the weather was nice because we had to eat outdoors—there was nowhere else to go: Liz said she couldn't have all of us tramping all over the kitchen and Jess had told us she definitely didn't want anyone eating and drinking in the library.

I was glad I had to run the gardening business; it excused me from the decorating rota. They'd started early that morning, about six, and it looked like it was going to go on until the following night at least.

I met Jess on the way to the kitchen. We knocked on the door and Liz, looking very flustered, handed us a plate piled high with sandwiches. I wasn't surprised she looked flustered, she was catering for a big party that night too—Rachel, who was managing the catering business, had arranged it without realising the whole house would be disrupted from the decorating.

Jess asked, 'Where shall we sit?'

'Let's go out on the front steps.' I loved to sit there, looking over the smooth lawn and hearing the noise of the house behind us. Will, Ruth, Gemma and Josh were already out on the steps; their hair and clothes white and dusty from stripping off the old wallpaper.

'Here they come! It's the skivers.' That was Josh.

I laughed. 'I'm not skiving, done a full day's work.'

'Me too,' said Jess. 'How would you like to teach that lot for the day?'

Gemma smiled. 'Good point!'

We sat down and began eating. Paul came up the path towards us. He'd just got an important web-designing contract and found it easier to work away from the disruptions of the house so he'd moved his computer to the gatehouse. There was a proper office there, as peaceful as any office could be. I'd been known to use it myself.

Jess moved her legs so he could pass. 'Been working late?' she asked.

'Something like that,' he answered and hurried into the house.


In the early hours of the next morning I was awoken by a knocking noise. Tom opened the door and I heard George's voice, although I couldn't tell what he was saying. When Tom came back in, he said, 'Elijah wants us all down in the library now. George won't tell me what it's about.'

It felt really early and it was hard to open my eyes and look at my watch. Three thirty. I couldn't think of anything that would be worth getting up for at that time.

In the library everyone was squashed together; two to each chair, on the floor, on the windowsills, leaning against the walls. I pushed my way to the back of the room and leant against a bookshelf.

Rachel came in with Tammy and Louise. She found a small space at the front for them to sit on the floor then she came and stood next to me. Rebecca arrived carrying a half-awake Becky. Gemma stood up so she could have the chair in front of me and perched on the arm. Becky snuggled down on Rebecca's knee and went back to sleep.

There was hardly any talking and everyone looked half asleep. I was drifting off myself so I didn't hear Elijah come in, but when he spoke it was so loud it made me jump.

'First I want to read John fifteen, eighteen to twenty.'

Becky stirred in her mother's arms but didn't wake up.

'"If the world hates you, be aware that it hated me before it hated you. If you belonged to the world, the world would love you as its own. Because you do not belong to the world, but I have chosen you out of the world—therefore the world hates you. Remember the word that I said to you, 'Servants are not greater than their master.' If they persecuted me, they will persecute you; if they kept my word, they will keep yours also".'

Elijah seemed excited; he was pacing the floor even though there wasn't much room to move about.

'What can we learn from John? Well, we already know that we have been chosen to serve the Lord by living here in this special community, this *family*, and, John tells us, because of that the world will hate us. The world will persecute us. We must always, always remember that. We must learn to walk amongst them without becoming contaminated—that is the only way that we can follow our mission to save some of them from themselves. Some of you already do that: Josh, George and Andrea go out on the streets, handing out pamphlets and talking to those who believe themselves lost, in order that we can save them. We run three successful businesses. All those involved have had to learn to interact and yet keep themselves apart at the same time.'

Elijah stopped and stood perfectly still for a moment; he seemed to be thinking what he needed to say next.

'But we must do more than that. We must prepare for a time when the world will take action against us—we can be certain that such a time will come. It may be that we will be attacked as we go about our holy work. It may be that they come to our community, our *home* and attempt to hurt us. There are so many devious ways they could do that. They could close down our home and separate us. They could fabricate crimes and put us in prison. They could even take our children away from us. We can never predict what form their evil will take.

'Some of you will know about my time in America. I lived in a religious community in Louisiana. What a wonderful place that was, they worked hard and they prayed hard.

'Then the American police decided to close it down. Forced their way in with guns in their hands. Accused the leader of a variety of crimes – all of them fabricated.'

The atmosphere had become tense; people were straining forward to catch every word.

Elijah carried on. 'It's happened again. In Montana this time. A small community, one like ours, filled with people like us, has been totally destroyed by the American police. Guns. Missiles. Fires. No one left alive.'

He pointed down at Tammy and Louise seated at his feet.

'Even young children like these two. Slaughtered.'

The two girls began to cry. Rachel tried to reach her children but couldn't find a way through the crowded room. She wiped away a tear and I put my arm around her shoulders to comfort her.

It was several moments before Elijah lifted his head and began speaking again.

'There's been a lot of coverage in the press and on TV about religious communities. Paul has seen it on the internet. They're saying that the group in Montana were armed. Saying that they had cellars filled with guns and ammunition. Saying that they'd planned to take over a nearby town and use it as a base to extend their operation through the States and into this country. Some of the extreme British papers are trying to scare people into believing that it's going to happen here. They are asking for armed police to storm our communities and split us up, just in case.'

You could almost touch the panic in the room until Elijah raised his hand.

'I don't think we need to worry too much yet. We know how the British operate, it's a more softly, softly approach and they're unlikely to burst in on us yet. But,' he paused and looked round, 'there are no guarantees and we must be ready for any eventuality.'

Elijah knelt down between Tammy and Louise and put a hand on each of their heads.

'Look at them. We need to protect this innocence from anyone who would seek to do them harm. They may use force, they may use violence, they could use guns. Or they may take our children away and indoctrinate them, filling them with their filth and forcing them to live their lives without the comfort of the Lord. We cannot predict the ways of this evil world.'

He stood up again. 'We need to look how we can improve the defences of this house so we can protect ourselves from any possible attack.

'I've spent the time since we got the news about Montana talking to George and Paul, but we haven't had time to come up with any detailed plans. We've decided to take more time on this, we don't want to rush into it and make mistakes. It's going to be a couple of days before we are ready to share our ideas on security arrangements with you. One thing I'm fairly sure on is that we will have to shelve our search for more sleeping accommodation for a while. This is much more important than that.'

Josh stood up. 'How can we help?'

Elijah smiled. 'I was just coming to that, Josh. We need the Lord to give us the wisdom to make the right choices, to find the best path for our own protection. So

I want you all to spend as much time as possible praying that God guides us to make the right decisions.

'We three are going to be fasting over this time so that our minds aren't distracted by trivialities. I don't believe in *making* others fast, but I hope that most of you will also find the strength to fast as well so that your minds are clear and focussed on your prayers.'

# Eighteen

I always found it hard to fast and the next two days seemed to take forever. It didn't seem difficult to the others to go hungry, but my mind kept wandering to food and, for some reason, all the shopkeepers seemed to be celebrating birthdays and anniversaries; they kept offering me chocolates and pieces of cake. I told them I was on a strict diet.

The decorating was to be left until after the decisions were made—it meant that the house would be disrupted for a while longer but no one really minded. Other jobs were being left too, but I couldn't let my customers down. I did my rounds as quickly as possible though, so I could get back to the house and be with the others.


We'd been told that Elijah would be talking to us around seven pm, but he wasn't ready so we sat outside talking for a while. About nine it became cooler so we went into the house, sitting anywhere we could find space. As I sat down at the bottom of the stairs, I heard shouting and I was surprised to see Becky run out of the library. She saw me and climbed on my knee.

'Why aren't you in bed, young lady?'

'Everyone else was staying up so Mummy said I could stay up too.'

'So what was all the shouting about?'

'Mummy's cross. Why is she so cross?' she asked.

'I don't know. What did you do?'

'I didn't do nothing.'

Jess was passing and must have heard what Becky said.

'I think you asked too many questions, Becky.'

'But I wanted to know the answers. Anyway, Mummy was cross before I started asking questions. Why's Mummy keep being cross today, Liam?'

'She's probably tired and hungry.'

'Why?'

'Because we've been busy praying and she hasn't had any dinner.'

'She hasn't been having any lunch or breakfast either. Lots of people haven't. Why's that?'

'So we can pray really hard. Sometimes not eating helps you pray better. We've all not been eating so we could pray that Elijah finds some good ways to make the house safer.'

'I have my dinner before I say my prayers. Should I leave my dinner when I want to pray?'

'No, you need your dinner because you're a growing girl.'

'I think Mummy needs her dinner too. Then she wouldn't be so cross.'

George came out of the office and asked us all to go into the library. I picked Becky up and we squeezed ourselves into a corner. Then Elijah came in. Becky was trying to whisper in my ear so I told her to be quiet. She put on a sulky face but stopped whispering as Elijah cleared his throat.

'Sorry it's taken so long. We wanted to be sure we were doing the right things. It's very late so I'll just read out the list of measures and who we want to work on them. We can talk about it all in Circle Time tomorrow.

1. No strangers to be allowed past the gatehouse. Business visitors will be seen in the gatehouse office.
2. Someone to be on duty in the gatehouse day and night. Josh to set up a rota.

3. An intercom to be installed by ourselves between the office and the gatehouse. Josh to arrange.
4. Telephone lines to be removed from the house so we can't be bugged. As we need the lines for the businesses and the Internet, we'll have them transferred to the gatehouse. Josh to arrange.
5. All outside doors to be kept locked at all times. All adults to wear keys round their necks and to remember to lock doors after them. George to arrange.
6. The children are not to play outside unsupervised. Jess to discuss with children and parents the best way to arrange this.
7. Everyone to do self-defence training—Will to investigate training packages.
8. Barbed wire to be put on all unobserved walls and fences. Jim to arrange—volunteers please give your names to him.
9. Paul to research on Internet whether we can obtain suitable weapons to defend ourselves. We're not sure how realistic this is so, once the research has been done, we'll have a community meeting to discuss the pros and cons.
10. Tom to investigate the potential of the cellars as a safe place to hide.
11. Paul and Elijah to write an escape plan to be used if we get enough advance notice of problems.

The sub-committee that I was on met in the library to talk about a safe place to hide. There had been so many meetings lately that one of the long tables from the dining room had been brought in permanently. The children's desks and chairs were pushed to one side for the meetings.

Elijah, Paul, George, Tom and Jess were on the committee and Ruth was taking the minutes. Tom had looked at the cellar and found it was in quite good condition. He'd discovered that it had a reinforced ceiling from the time during the war when it was used as a bomb shelter. There were four large rooms, a pantry and a basic toilet and washbasin. The electricity needed sorting out but he was sure Jim could do that. He thought it would be very suitable.

Paul said there was a problem; the cellar door was in the hallway, directly facing the front door. He thought that if anyone came looking for us they'd be down there like a shot. Everyone was quiet, trying to think of a way round it. Tom half raised his hand in the air and spoke at the same time.

'There's another way into the cellar, you know.'

Everyone stared at him with surprise. Paul was the one who asked, 'Where?'

'There's a door at the back of the pantry. I know because I was the one who locked it to stop anyone getting into there. The stairs are in a dreadful condition and someone could easily get hurt. I locked the door and blocked the entrance from the cellar to the stairs with an old wardrobe.

'When was this?' Elijah asked.

'Quite a few years ago. I'd almost forgotten about it.'

'Did you talk to me about it?'

'I might have done but I honestly can't remember.'

'I don't think that matters, Elijah,' said Paul, 'what matters is that we have a potential solution here. Could you make the stairs safe, Tom?'

'No problem.'

'And have you got the key to the locked door?'

'I think it's in the key safe, marked 'pantry'. I'll check later. If not I'll force the lock and fit a new one.'

'We'd have to block the cellar doorway in the hall too and hide any signs it was there.'

'The hallway could do with decorating anyway. I'll make a start on it when I've sorted the stairs down into the cellar,' said Tom.

'We'll get some volunteers to help, Tom, don't worry that you'll be stuck with doing all that,' said Paul.

'And I'll hang on to the key for the pantry door into the cellar,' said Elijah, 'don't want anyone wandering down there by mistake. Tom, I want you to make sure you hand it back to me whenever you've used it.'

Tom nodded.

'Thanks for that, Tom, that's really helpful,' Paul said.

Ruth was still scribbling down what had happened.

I had a question in my head that wouldn't go away so I waited for Ruth to finish writing and then I said, 'What will happen after we go down there. We won't be able to come back up again, will we? They'll be waiting for us.'

Elijah took the pen from Ruth's hand and said, 'Let's make this off the record, shall we?' He nodded towards the door and Paul went to lock it.

Elijah went on. 'We've prayed a lot about this particular matter. It might be that we can get away with hiding down in the cellar for a while and pretending that we've gone away. But we might not. So the question is what happens then?'

We looked at each other and then back at Elijah.

'The Lord has told me that it is better for us to take our own lives and go to him, than to fall into the hands of the devil.'

Ruth held her hand up. 'Surely that can't be true, Elijah. You're talking about suicide and that's a sin. How could God want us to commit a sin like that?'

'Think about it Ruth, all of you. What if one of our young impressionable children was taken from us and put into some home to live amongst those with no morals or beliefs? Imagine our little Becky being subject to those influences, being led away from the path of righteousness and given to the devil for his own purposes. That would surely be a greater sin, wouldn't it?'

Paul spoke up. 'It would be bad for all of us but absolutely horrendous for our children. They are so innocent. Think of the things that can happen to young children out there—falling into the hands of perverts, being sexually abused via the internet, sold into prostitution.'

I thought about Becky living in a home like the one I'd lived in, about her not having enough to eat, lying in bed at night praying that she wouldn't be dragged out of bed to be punished for something she hadn't done or pulling the covers over her head so she couldn't hear the arguing downstairs. I couldn't bear that. But I couldn't think of anyone intentionally taking her life either. I had to ask. 'How would we die? Would the children suffer before they died?'

Elijah put his hands together and bent his head towards the tip of his fingers. 'Trust me. And Paul and George. We'd sort it out. We'd make sure no one suffered, that it was all very quick. It's not something you need to take responsibility for.'

'We hope and pray it won't come to that,' George said 'and we promise that the situation would have to be really desperate before we even considered it.'

'So we're asking that the three of you forget this conversation. It's just a plan that we've made in case we need it. As always we will pray for guidance before we take that step and be assured it will only be if it is the Lord's will. God never gives us more than we can bear.'

We nodded our heads. Ruth picked up her pen and we went on with the meeting.

Tom was to ask Jim to help him improve the cellar, buy the necessary furniture, put in new stairs behind the pantry door, brick up the door in the hallway and redecorate so it didn't seem that there'd ever been a doorway there.

Someone was needed to oversee the work and I felt a thrill of pride go through me when Elijah said I would be the best person for the job. He said he knew that I had a lot of responsibilities already, but he trusted me to be able to fit other work in.

The meeting ended and I tried to push the idea of suicide to the back of my mind. Sometimes I managed it, but at other times a picture of Becky lying pale and still would come rushing to my thoughts.

# Nineteen

Mr Kumar told me a woman had been asking about me. He'd given her one of our flower cards with the telephone number on, but she'd said it was personal and she didn't like ringing. He'd also asked her to leave her number, but she said she'd rather keep an eye out for me. He'd given her my delivery times.

Just then he said, 'Oh look, that's her.'

I looked through the window, but she didn't seem familiar. I went outside.

'Mr Kumar says you've been looking for me.'

She turned around. 'Hello, Liam.'

I stared. My mother was standing in front of me, looking happier and healthier than I'd ever seen her. I tried to speak but the words were whirling round my mind so fast I couldn't catch hold of one long enough to force it out of my dry mouth. I put my hand flat against the shop window to hold myself steady.

'It's me. Kirsty.'

I swallowed hard. Of course it was Kirsty. Or it might have been Kelly, but only my sisters could look so much like our mother. I managed to croak, 'You've grown up.'

Then I felt stupid. Of course she'd grown up. The last time I'd seen her was fifteen years before when she'd been fourteen.

She laughed. 'So have you.'

We stood and stared at each other for what felt like forever until someone pushed their way past me. We were blocking the pavement.

I spoke without thinking. 'There's a café down here. Let's go and have a cup of coffee and talk.'

I set off and she followed. Then the usual problem came to my mind. 'I haven't any money on me. I haven't even got a float today.'

'That's okay, I'll pay.' She laughed. 'I'll just add it to the fiver you owe me from last time I saw you.'

'Sorry, Kirsty. I did some bad things round that time.'

'I didn't mind, honest. I was glad that you were getting yourself some freedom. You didn't belong in that house.'

When the two coffees were on the table in front of us I began staring again. I couldn't get over how much like mum she looked.

'Bet you're thinking how fat I am. It's because of the baby.'

I hadn't even noticed.

'You're having a baby? Wow, fantastic. When's it due?'

'Got another three months to go. It was the baby that made me want to find you. It started me thinking about how important family is. I want my baby to know all his family.'

I didn't know what to say. Kirsty's family. My family. I'd hardly thought about them as people since I'd left. Hadn't wanted to. But I'd carried the pain and anger around with me. In the beginning I'd played with it in the same way you play with a painful tooth, vowing to leave it alone, but then finding yourself touching it with your tongue so that it makes you wince and brings tears to your eyes. I'd had to bury it very deep when I joined The Community so that it didn't contaminate my new life.

The Community! I'd forgotten them. How could I do that? I was forbidden to have contact with my old family. I pushed my chair back, ready to leave.

'I shouldn't be here. I've got to go.'

She looked like she was about to cry and grabbed hold of my hand.

'Please don't go. I haven't seen you for years and if Auntie Mary hadn't spotted you that day I'd never have found you.'

Mum's face pleaded with me to stay. I remembered trying to look after Mum and the kids so they didn't cry. I always wanted to make things right for them, but I'd been so young and Dad had been much stronger than me.

'Alright, I'll stay for a few minutes, but then I have to go and I won't ever be able to see you again.'

I sat down again, took a tissue from my pocket and handed it to her so she could wipe her eyes.

'Why not? Why are you talking about leaving and never seeing me again? It can't be anything I've done; we've only been together five minutes in fifteen years.'

How could I explain? 'I live in a religious community. It's against the rules to have personal links with the outside world.'

'A *religious* community? You? How did you end up there? And anyway, I thought you worked for a flower business.'

'The business belongs to the community—I run it for them. They took me in a few years ago when I'd hit rock bottom with my drinking. It's a brilliant place, Kirst, I'm really happy there.'

'I'm glad you're happy but what have they got against me? I wouldn't do anything to harm them or you.'

'It's not you; we just cut our ties with the outside world because The Community and God are more important than anything else. It's my new family and I'm not supposed to have anything to do with my old family.'

I could see she was confused but I couldn't explain it any other way. She tried again.

'It can't do any harm for us to spend some time together. Why can't we have a nice chat and then perhaps you can come over to Whalley to see me?'

'Sorry, doesn't work like that. Sounds like you're doing alright though. Whalley is a nice part of the world.'

'Yeah. I've had this lovely little house for about five years. Matt moved in with me a couple of years ago. We're very happy.'

'So Matt's the daddy of your new baby then?'

'Yeah, he's as excited as I am.'

Now I'd decided to stay and talk for a while, I thought I might as well find out about the others.

'How's Kelly? What's she doing?'

'She's fine. Nursing, like me. We did our training together but now she's works at Manchester Royal and I'm at Burnley General.'

'And Steven?'

'Oh, he's in Manchester too. Working as an accountant.'

Good old Steve. An accountant. I could really imagine that. I was glad they were all doing well.

'Suppose I should ask about Auntie Mary and Uncle Bill.'

It's funny how I still resented them even after all that time. Jess would have put her hand on my shoulder and said, 'Do unto others...' Or maybe not: I remembered how she felt about her parents.

'They moved over to Southport after we all left. Uncle Bill died a couple of years ago. Auntie Mary found it hard for a while, but she's doing alright now. Likes to go out on day trips to various places. That's how she saw you, she'd come over to do some shopping.'

Poor old Bill. He hadn't been that bad and had tried to treat me fairly. But perhaps he was better off with The Lord than Auntie Mary. Kirsty hesitated, then said, 'Dad's out of prison.'

I didn't want to know but Kirsty seemed determined to tell me about him once she'd brought the subject up.

'He came out about six years ago. I've seen him a couple of times, but we don't have much in common. All he wants to talk about is how badly the police and the courts have treated him when Mum's death was nothing but a tragic accident.'

The pain and anger began to bubble inside me.

'Let's not talk about him. How are you really? Are you happy?'

'I am. I'm really happy. Matt's great and we're really excited about the baby. I just wish we could spend more time with you.'

'I'm sorry, I truly am, but I've made this commitment to The Community. They've made my life worth living and I owe them everything. I can't go against what they believe, it's all too important to me. '

She nodded reluctantly. 'If it's so important to you.'

'It is Kirsty, it is. It's my whole life.'

'Alright, I accept that, but let me give you my address just in case you ever need anything.'

She pulled an envelope from her bag, took the letter out then pushed the envelope in my shirt pocket. I put my hand up to stop her, but she looked so upset I let her.

'You've got to understand, Kirsty, I can't contact you again. Look after yourself and the baby. You're a very special person, always remember that.'

She looked so sad. I bent down and kissed the top of her head. Then I left the café and didn't look back—if I had I'd never have got out of there.


All the way back to The Larches images flickered through my mind. Nice ones of playing with Kirsty, Kelly and Steven in that tiny bedroom filled with two sets of bunk beds. Not so nice ones of living in Uncle Bill and Auntie Mary's house. And a horrible one of Mum lying at the bottom of the stairs with blood trickling down her face from a huge gash that I'd tried to hold together with three tiny plasters. She'd been dying, but I didn't understand that then. I forgot about the envelope with the address on. All those pictures in my head must have pushed it out of my mind.

Mrs Jenkinson owned the newsagent's in Station Road. It was going to be her daughter's birthday and she'd asked me to make a special bouquet for her. I'd written the order on a piece of paper and put it in my pocket, thinking that I'd let Jonathan help with this one and, when I got back to the house, he was talking to Elijah. I pulled the piece of paper out of my shirt pocket to show him, but as I took it out Kirsty's envelope caught on it and floated down through the air to land at Elijah's feet. I tried to grab it but Elijah got to it first. He was about to hand it to me, but then he must have read the name on it.

'What's this?'

'It's just one of my customers. She wanted the address writing on the card.'

'Kirsty Donnelly. *Donnelly*. Same last name as you. That's a bit of a coincidence, isn't it? Is she any relation?'

'No, I told you, she's a customer.'

Elijah's eyes burnt into mine. I was useless at lying.

'Let's go and talk about this in the office.'

In the office he sat down and waved his hand for me to sit opposite him. He put the envelope on the desk, midway between us.

'Right, Liam. Look me in the eye and tell me this Kirsty Donnelly is no relation to you.'

I looked into his face; I felt like he could read my thoughts, that he knew where I'd been and who I'd been with. The truth came out of my mouth straightaway.

'It's my sister. I met her whilst I was on my rounds. I've told her I can't see her again.'

'You've gone against everything we believe in.' He banged his fist against the desk. 'She is not your sister. Not any more. Your family is here and you have betrayed them. And the Lord.'

'She's been looking for me. She's having a baby and wanted all her family to know. I've explained that I belong here and that I have a new family. I promise I won't ever see her again. I told her that and she's said she won't come after me.'

'And yet you kept her address in your pocket? How am I supposed to believe that you aren't planning to contact her again?'

'I swear I wasn't planning to see her again. She put that address in there and I forgot. I just forgot.' I buried my head in my hands. How could I make him believe me?

'Don't tell me any more lies, Liam. I can see that we can't trust you any more. I want you to wait outside while I think about how to deal with this. I don't want you to talk to anyone. Do you understand?'

I nodded and then went to sit on a chair in the hallway. Jonathan was still out there. He looked like he was going to come over and talk to me, but I waved him away.

It was warm in the hallway, but through the window I could see the trees lashing backwards and forwards in the wind. There were black clouds in the sky as though a storm was about to start. Still, I'd rather have been outside in a storm than inside in the storm that was brewing around me.

After about fifteen minutes Elijah called me back in.

'Right, Liam. I feel I can't trust you to go out on your rounds anymore. I'm going to ask Ian to do the deliveries in future. I'll get Jonathan to help him; he already knows the route and the customers. And, for now, you can make a start on the cellar while we work out whether you can continue to be involved in the gardening. I want you to go down there now and I don't expect to see you up here until dinner. Look on it as your punishment.'

It was horrible down in that cellar. It wasn't the dirt or the spiders or even the scratching noises that I suspected were caused by rats. It was dark and musty and I kept feeling that the walls were moving inwards to trap me. I was so used to being out in the open air that I found it hard to breathe and my chest felt tighter and tighter as time went on.

I started work in the farthest room and began working my way through the piles of boxes, sorting out the rubbish from what might be useful. I hadn't brought any rubbish bags down with me and I daren't go back up for any so I could only make big piles of things.

I don't know how long I'd been down there when I heard Jess's voice.

'Liam. Liam. Where are you?'

'In here.'

She peered round the doorway and then ran towards me to give me a big hug.

'Jonathan said you were in trouble and you've been sent down here for punishment. What happened?'

I explained about Kirsty and meeting up with her.

'I believe you, Liam. You've committed your life to this place. You wouldn't let us down like that. Come on, let's go and talk to Elijah.'

I followed her up the steep steps and into Elijah's office. He stood up when we walked in and he looked as if he was about to speak but Jess got in first.

'Liam told you the truth about his sister. He hadn't planned to meet her, she came to find him. What was he supposed to do?'

'He was supposed to turn and walk away from her.' Elijah banged his fist on the table. 'That's his commitment, his promise to us. No contact whatsoever.'

'That's not being realistic, Elijah. He was faced with a difficult situation and he dealt with it in the only way he knew how. There was nothing else he could do.'

Elijah turned to me. He looked so angry I thought he might explode, but he spoke in a controlled voice.

'Go and sit in the outer office while I have a word with Jess.'

For the second time that day I followed Elijah's orders and waited outside for him. But this time I could hear what he thought as he shouted at Jess.

'What's going on between you and Liam?'

'I don't know what you mean.'

'Oh yes you do. You're all over him, sitting next to him at meals, gossiping in corners. Now you're standing up for him against me. I know you Jess; you don't do things like that for nothing.'

'There's nothing going on. Not in the way that you're thinking. He's a friend, a brother, just like everyone else here.'

There was a silence, then Elijah spoke again.

'That's not how it appears to me.'

'I don't *want* him. I told you, it's not like that. Liam's the last person I'd be interested in the way you mean.'

'I don't want to talk to you about Liam anymore—I've told you what I think. Bring him in; we'll sort something out about what he does round here.'

Jess appeared in the office doorway. She'd never looked more beautiful, but I knew for certain that any dream I might have had about us getting together would never come true. She didn't see me as anything but a friend or a brother. I'd heard her say it. The death of my dreams, but not of my love. That would last forever.

# Twenty

The next few weeks were very difficult. Somehow word had got out about me meeting Kirsty and a lot of people were very angry about it. They believed I could have prevented it, but even though I thought about it over and over I couldn't find any way for things to have been different.

Elijah had agreed to allow me to carry on doing the deliveries, on condition that Jonathan went out with me. That was fine and in many ways Jonathan made my life a lot easier; the problem was I'd developed my own ways of doing things. Jonathan, being a typical teenager, kept coming up with new ideas for improvement and I didn't have the strength to disagree. He'd made up a new order form which had no logic at all and was very difficult to fill in. He'd also changed our route to make it more efficient, but it actually meant that we retraced our steps three times and it added another thirty minutes to deliveries. I was tense and what made it worse was that I no longer had precious time by myself as I drove along the country roads. I started having sleeping problems and felt exhausted all the time. It was like I was stranded in the fog and couldn't think of a way to make things better. In the outside world people would have said I needed a holiday, but there were no holidays at The Larches.

One morning, when I stood up from my breakfast, I felt very dizzy and I sat down again with a bump. Ian told me to go back to bed: he'd do the deliveries for me.

I climbed into bed, closed my eyes and the next thing I knew Josh was sitting on the side of the bed, asking if I felt better.

'Wha… what time is it?'

'It's four thirty. Dinner will be soon. Do you want to get up for it?'

I felt alright, in fact a great deal better than I'd felt for a while.

'Yeah, okay. Just give me a few minutes to come round. If there's no problems when I stand up, I'll see you down there.'

Josh closed the door and I looked at the ceiling. Hoping the dizziness had gone I pushed myself into a sitting position and thought about how I felt; still a little sleepy, but no dizziness as yet. I couldn't believe I'd slept all day, but it had done the trick. I swung my legs over the edge of the mattress and sat staring out of the window. Definitely no dizziness.

The world outside looked brighter than it had done in a while. The sky was a soft inviting blue and the leaves were a new paintbox green. I did want to get up, especially as I was feeling very hungry.

At dinner Will asked if I was up to Circle Time. It was going to be a games night, nothing too taxing. Will thought it might make me feel better and I said it sounded like a good idea.

It didn't make me feel better and it definitely wasn't a good idea.


'We're going to play Touchdown. Tammy, Louise, Becky and Laura, come and stand here so you don't get hurt in the rush. Gideon, do you want to play or is it a bit risky for you?'

'I'll be careful, George, promise.'

'OK. For those who have forgotten this is the way it works. Whenever I call out a direction you run that way. When I say Touchdown you lie down. The last one down and the one farthest away is out. Right, here we go.

'North.'

I ran towards the window.

'South.'

I turned and raced in the other direction.

'East.'

I followed the crowd.

'South... North... West... Touchdown.'

I flung myself to the floor. My right side was against Josh, my foot touched Ruth, my nose was in Ian's armpit. Will was out, as was Rachel.

'East.'

I scrambled up and ran with the crowd.

'North... South... North... West... East... Touchdown.'

I had my head in the small of Ruth's back, my eyes on a level with Gideon's shoes, one of my knees touching Gemma's nose.

Paul and Rebecca were out.

'North... East... West... East... West... South... Touchdown.'

I threw myself down next to Tom. Jess landed on top of me, her face next to mine. The heavy heat of her breast warmed my arm, her soft stomach curved against my hip, her legs entangled with mine. Her breath was sweet in my nose, her hair was silk on my cheek. I was drowning in Jess. I prayed, literally prayed, that I could stay there forever.

Someone was out.

'North.'

I was the last up.

'South.'

I was still heading north, running against the crowd. I turned just as the next instruction was called.

'East.'

I stumbled. I wanted to hurry, but my legs wouldn't do what they were told.

'South.'

I needed a compass. Which way was South?

'West... North... East... West... South... East.'

I was always one instruction behind everyone else. Sometimes I was a hazard blocking their path. Sometimes I was a lonely figure stumbling in the wrong direction.

'Touchdown.'

I was glad I was out because I didn't have to try anymore. I sat in a corner not-watching the game. My nerve endings were tingling and my thoughts raced, but I didn't dare admit, even to myself, what was actually running through my mind.

I decided to take the following day off as well. I got up about two and wandered into the kitchen.

'Have you anything to eat, Liz, I'm starving.'

She shook her finger at me.

'In my day poorly folk stayed in bed and said they weren't hungry.'

'Aw, Liz, it's not that sort of poorly. I'm feeling run down, need to build up my strength.'

'I was only teasing, love. What about some cereal and a banana to keep you going till dinner.'

'Sounds good to me.'

I went into the Social Room and sat near the window. Jess was out on the lawn with the younger children—it looked like she was telling them a story, struggling to hold the page still enough to read against the breeze.

I lectured myself about needing to change the way I felt about her. I repeated the prayer that always comes to my mind when I find life difficult.

'God grant us the serenity to accept the things we cannot change, the courage to change the things we can, and the wisdom to know the difference.'

I knew I needed strength to do this because I couldn't live my life dreaming of someone I couldn't have.

# Twenty One

*Afternoon Assembly*

Elijah opened up the Bible and read, "Then God said, 'Let us make mankind in our image, according to our likeness; and let them have dominion over the fish of the sea, and over the birds of the air, and over the cattle, and over all the wild animals of the earth, and over every creeping thing that creeps upon the earth.' So God created mankind in his image, in the image of God he created them; male and female he created them. God blessed them, and God said to them, 'Be fruitful and multiply, and fill the earth and subdue it'."

Elijah put down the Bible and looked around at the assembled community.

'That's what it says in the first book of Moses. We've set up this community to follow God's word and yet we aren't doing what he says. How can we replenish the earth and subdue it when we aren't following the basic instruction to multiply?

'When we set up this Community we said we didn't want established couples and didn't think any further than that. Now here we are, eight years later, with more than sixty members and we still haven't taken the first step towards increasing our numbers in a natural way.

'I've asked God how we can multiply and He has said to me that we should choose couples from amongst our members. Couples who we know will always put God and the Community before themselves. If God blesses their union then we will be able to multiply from within. Bring children into this world who will be truly blessed because they will have come from the love of God and not from animal desires.'

112

Elijah put both hands on the table and looked down to the floor for a moment. Then he lifted his head and looked up to the ceiling.

'God has asked me to find five couples from within this Community. It's a difficult task, but with His help I know I will choose well. My plan is to spend the next twenty four hours identifying ten members and then putting them into couples. I want you to add your prayers to mine over this time. We aren't having an Afternoon Assembly tomorrow so I will pin the list up on the hallway notice board tomorrow at five thirty so that you can know who has been chosen.'


I didn't expect my name to be on the list, but I still wanted to know who was there. I'd been working in the far field that afternoon and finished at about twenty past five. I had time to wash my hands and then walk over to the house to see the list as soon as it went up.

I put the tools in the shed and went into the first greenhouse to wash my hands. As I stood at the sink I felt something brush past my legs. It was Methuselah; he must have followed me in. The last time he'd been shut in the greenhouse he'd done a lot of damage, mainly knocking things off shelves, but he'd also pulled a couple of plants up. I had to catch him.

Methuselah might have been old, but he could still act like a young kitten when he felt like it. First he ran to the far end of the greenhouse dodging from side to side each time I approached him. It was hot in there—I could feel the sweat in my armpits and my mouth was dry. Eventually I chased him towards the door, but then he jumped up on a shelf, pacing from side to side, his eyes big as he watched me walking towards him. He stretched out a clawed paw as I put my hand under his stomach to lift him down, then he sunk first one set of claws and then the other into my hand. As I put my other hand under his bottom to hold his weight he tried to bite my chin and I had to hold my head up high to keep out of his reach. I opened the door with my elbow and threw him down on the floor, putting my foot out to stop him getting back in. I stood and looked at the damage he'd done. Both hands were covered in scratches, a couple of which were bleeding. I decided to clean them up in the house; I wasn't going to risk Methuselah getting back in the greenhouse.

My heart was beating hard as I walked towards the house. I told myself that it was because this was such an important day for The Community but, to be honest, a little voice in my head was saying 'Maybe… maybe Elijah would put me with Rebecca, Ruth, Gemma or Andrea. I thought about what that would be like. Might be nice to have someone to share my life with, to have babies with, to have people saying, 'Liam and Ruth,' or 'Gemma and Liam.' But it wouldn't happen, I wasn't important enough, hadn't been there long enough.

The little voice started again. 'What if Elijah puts you with Jess?' I shook my head hard. 'Don't start down that road again, Liam. That's just being silly. Jess will be with Elijah. Definitely!'

It was about quarter to six when I got to the house. The hallway was empty apart from Jess who was standing in front of the noticeboard, her finger pointing at something on one of the notices. She pulled her hand away, stepped back, then peered at the notice again as if checking what it said.

As I was about to speak I saw her turn and run towards the stairs. She didn't say anything, probably didn't even see me for the tears running down her face. I wondered whether to go after her, but I thought it best to leave her to recover. She didn't like showing her emotions.

I found the list. My name *was* on it. It said:

Couples

Elijah & Rebecca
Liam & Jess
Paul & Ruth
Tom & Gemma
Will & Andrea

It had happened, but I couldn't believe it. I was going to marry Jess. I just didn't know how to feel. It was like every dream I ever had. To be with Jess. But it was also like every nightmare. I'd heard her say she didn't want to be with me. Marriage, even in a place like The Larches, was a big commitment, it would involve us sharing a room and sleeping together. And making love! All the time I would know that she didn't really want to be with me. Not in that way.

I went and locked myself in the toilet so no one could see how confused I was feeling. Josh came and knocked on the door after a while to check I was alright. I told him my stomach was upset—well it was true, my stomach was churning away each time I thought about the wedding.

# Twenty Two

*Minutes of the Marriage Sub-Committee*

Present:
Elijah, Rebecca, George, Paul, Ruth (Minute Secretary), Liam, Jess, Tom, Gemma, Liz, Will, Andrea, Rachel, Josh, Jim

1. Wedding
1.1 Date:
Wedding to be held in 6 weeks time on Thursday 6 April at 2pm.
1.2 Ceremony:
Ceremony to be written and carried out by George. Elijah and Paul to be consulted as and when necessary.
1.3 Women's outfits:
Rachel to discuss the design with the five women involved, then obtain patterns and material by mail order. Rachel to be main dressmaker, with help as necessary from the others.
1.4 Men's outfits:
Rachel to oversee the men's choice from mail order catalogue to ensure that they go with the women's outfits.
1.5 Flowers:
Liam to organise the flowers—home-grown if possible, but bought from alternative source if necessary.
1.6 Music:
Choice to be made by George, Paul and Josh. Josh to play guitar for ceremony and at reception party.
1.7 Food:
Liz to produce celebration buffet for after ceremony. No expense to be spared.

2. After Wedding

2.1 Accommodation:

Rachel and George had inspected the attics. There were 6 bedrooms and a functional bathroom. There was a lot of rubbish up there but, once the rooms were cleared out, cleaned and decorated they would make good accommodation. It would also ease the pressure on the accommodation in the rest of the house.

2.2 Bedrooms:

Each couple would be responsible for their own room—clearing, cleaning and decorating. Materials to be obtained from Jim who agreed to ensure that we have sufficient supplies.

2.3 Bathroom:

Jim to check over and carry out any necessary improvements.

2.4 Materials:

Jess to order any necessary soft furnishings, e.g. curtains, bedding, from the mail order catalogue.

2.5 Furniture:

Paul to order beds, wardrobes, drawers and chairs from Internet.


3. Interim

3.1 Work:

The house to go into restricted work pattern until the wedding. All existing commitments to be met, but no more to be accepted until after the wedding. Jess to reduce the time she spends with the children, using other members as substitute teachers or giving the younger children project work that can be supervised by Jonathan. No more town missionary work.


I forced open the bedroom door. The room was quite small but there would be plenty of space for a bed, a wardrobe and a chest of drawers. It was late afternoon but the room was still light enough to work in. I was glad about that, I hated the sight of a lit bare bulb and we hadn't got any light fittings yet.

I ran my hand over one of the walls. It felt quite smooth and there weren't any obvious holes in it—I was a dab-hand with a paintbrush, but I'd never done any plastering and I was hoping that I wouldn't have to begin learning, I'd got enough on my plate without looking for more to worry about. There was a lot of rubbish so I took a black plastic bag from a roll on the floor and began filling it with pieces of paper and rotting books.

The handle turned and the door opened part way before it snagged on a pile of old cardboard. Jess put her hand round the door and waved a black plastic bag at me. She shouted through the gap. 'I was coming in to help, but it looks like you've locked me out.'

'I wouldn't do that to you. Hang on; I'll just pull this cardboard out.'

I tugged on the cardboard until it pulled free of the door, making me sit on the floor with a bump. I could feel myself blushing at making a fool of myself in front of Jess. She must have seen how embarrassed I was, but luckily she didn't say anything, just put out her hand to help me up. I blushed even more at the touch of her hand.

'Where do you want me to start?'

I looked round. It was such chaos that there was no logic to any of it.

'Just pick a pile.'

Jess sat down on the floor and began sorting through the rubbish. Then she found an old photo album and started flicking through the pages.

'Ah, look at this Liam.' She held the album up. 'It's an engagement photo.'

Two young people, side by side, in old-fashioned clothes and with serious faces. He held her right hand out supporting her left to show her sparkling ring to the camera.

Ruth opened the door and looked down at Jess. 'We think we've found the right design for our dresses. Do you want to come and look?'

Jess looked at me. 'Can you manage without me for a while?'

I nodded yes. Jess put the album on the floor and scrambled up to follow Ruth. 'See you in a little while.'

She closed the door behind her, leaving me alone. I picked up the album and looked through it: lots of pictures, most of them very different from the posed engagement photo. Quite a few had been taken at The Larches. As the pages turned I saw the young couple living their lives. After the engagement came the wedding. The man was in uniform so it must have been during the war. Then the children. A boy, a girl and then another boy; growing from chubby babies to grinning toddlers to sulky teenagers to adults with children of their own. At the back of the book were some photos that had never been stuck in the album. An elderly couple, holidaying in bright sunshine.

This was how it should happen. A couple falling in love and choosing to be together. Growing into a family and then back to a couple again to grow old together, watching from a distance as their children produced their own children.

But that wouldn't happen for me. For us. We'd been put together by Elijah whether we loved each other or not. When (or if) we had children, they would belong to the whole community, not just to us. They wouldn't go away to have homes of their own, they'd stay here, probably to be matched with a partner by Elijah or someone like him. It wasn't how I'd ever expected my marriage to be, but now I didn't have any choice in the matter.

I closed the album and pushed it to the bottom of the bag. I had to stop dreaming, my life had to follow the pattern Elijah had chosen for me. If I wanted to stay at The Larches, that is. And I did.

# Twenty Three

Late afternoon. Anyone looking through the windows to the outside world would see the heavy grey clouds that sent rain to beat against the windows. But no-one was interested in what was going on outside; they were too excited about the wedding. The partition between the Social Room and the Dining Room had been drawn back. The room was lit by many candles and the glow from the fire. Josh sat in a corner playing the guitar. Liam had put small glass vases of freesias around the room and their sweet scent decorated the air. Most of The Community was seated at the far ends of the room facing towards the middle where there was a small table covered with a red and gold cloth: in the centre stood a large silver candlestick with five smaller silver candlesticks forming a semi-circle at its base.

George came in wearing a light green collarless shirt and dark green trousers. He walked towards the table, placed a large white candle in the central candlestick and lit it, then he walked to the centre of the wall opposite the door and turned to face inward.

Next Gideon came in wearing a light blue collarless shirt with dark blue trousers. He carried five white candles which he put into the smaller candlesticks. He took his place to George's left.

Daniel and Jonathan entered dressed like Gideon. Daniel held five yellow roses. He placed one at the base of each small candlestick and Jonathan put ten golden rings as an outer semi-circle around the roses. They stood to the left of Gideon.

Becky, Louise and Tammy came in wearing pale pink cheesecloth—peasant blouses with full length tiered skirts. They were carrying small green baskets containing pink rose petals which they scattered on the floor around the table. Then they formed a line to George's right.

Elijah, Liam, Paul, Tom and Will walked through the door. They wore white collarless shirts and trousers. They stood in an evenly spaced semi-circle around the central table, facing George.

Next Rebecca, Jess, Ruth, Gemma and Andrea came in. They wore white cheesecloth peasant blouses and full length tiered skirts. They positioned themselves in the semi-circle next to their prospective partners.

George spoke. 'Could you each turn to face your intended partner and take their hands?'

Elijah faced Rebecca, Liam faced Jess, Paul faced Ruth, Tom faced Gemma, and Will faced Andrea. Becky lifted her hand and fluttered her fingers in a wave to her mother. Rebecca smiled back at her, but Elijah turned and glared until Becky looked down at the floor.

George began the ceremony with a passage from the first book of John.

"Beloved, let us love one another, because love is from God; everyone who loves is born of God and knows God. Whoever does not love does not know God, for God is love. ⁹God's love was revealed among us in this way: God sent his only Son into the world so that we might live through him. In this is love, not that we loved God but that he loved us and sent his Son to be the atoning sacrifice for our sins. Beloved, since God loved us so much, we also ought to love one another."

George paused for a moment and looked round the room. He smiled.

'John talks about love. We know about love, don't we? This room, this house is filled with love. Love for each other and for God. We've asked these ten people to represent that love, to *expand* that love by forming a special close bond. A bond which begins here in the sight of God and this community. A bond which, God willing, should bring forth children whom we can raise in the strength of this community's love. Children who can go forth and carry God's word out into the wider world, a world which so needs our love.

'Today these couples will be joined in marriage in a special ceremony, a ceremony which celebrates the threefold nature of their union—their union with each other, with this community and with God. First they will celebrate their joining together with the traditional symbol of a ring.

'Elijah, Liam, Paul, Tom and Will can you place the ring on the third finger of your partner's left hand.'

Each man took the ring and placed it part way on their partner's finger. Liam struggled a little because his hand was shaking.

'Now repeat after me: this ring symbolises the never ending circle of our union, our commitment to each other, to The Community and to God.'

The men repeated the words and then pushed the rings fully on to the women's fingers.

'Rebecca, Jess, Ruth, Gemma and Andrea, can you place the ring on the third finger of your partner's left hand.'

The women did so. Liam tried hard to stop his hand trembling but he couldn't manage to do so.

'Now repeat after me: this ring symbolises the never ending circle of our union, our commitment to each other, to The Community and to God.'

Liam looked into Jess's eyes as she spoke. The importance of this moment washed over him and he briefly thought of running and hiding from the consequences of this action. He didn't want to make Jess unhappy, but...

'I want each couple to take a rose and hold it together.'

The women each picked up a rose and held the stem with both hands. The men placed their hands on top of the women's.

'Like a flower, love is precious and delicate. It needs tender care to make it grow, to push through the soil into the light. Your love and care for each other will help this community to grow and expand, make it stronger to do the Lord's work.'

Becky walked round the circle taking the flowers from the couples. Then she returned to her place.

George moved towards the table, took a taper and lit it from the main candle. He held the taper in the air as he spoke.

'Let God's light shine on these unions.'

He handed the taper to Elijah. Elijah and Rebecca held the taper together to light a smaller candle, and then passed it to Liam and Jess. Liam marvelled at the firm strength of Jess's hand.

When all the candles were lit, George ended the ceremony.

'"Little children, let us love, not in word or speech, but in truth and action. [19]And by this we will know that we are from the truth and will reassure our hearts before him [20]whenever our hearts condemn us; for God is greater than our hearts, and he knows everything. [21]Beloved, if our hearts do not condemn us, we have boldness before God; [22]and we receive from him whatever we ask, because we obey his commandments and do what pleases him. And this is his commandment, that we should believe in the name of his Son Jesus Christ and love one another, just as he has commanded us." One John three, eighteen to twenty-three.'

*

124

At about nine thirty that night Elijah announced that it was time for the couples to retire. This was it. The moment I'd been worrying about. We made our way upstairs in single file. No one spoke until we reached the landing then we said goodnight to each other and hugged.

Jess opened the bedroom door and went inside. I followed her. When I closed the door behind me it sounded so loud. I leant back against the door and gazed round at the room. Our room. We'd painted the walls and furniture white; the curtains were a pale lemon. The only bright colour in the room was the patchwork quilt on the bed. Our bed. It seemed to be filling the room and I could see nothing else; even Jess disappeared.

I took a deep breath and went over to the window to close the curtains. I looked out at the night sky. The stars seemed to be looking down on me. I looked away from the sky and spotted the greenhouses. I wished I were in there working with the plants. Or even travelling through the night sky in a plane. Anywhere but in that room at that time. But I was there and had to face up to it. I pulled the curtains together and turned away from the window.

Jess was sitting on the bed. I thought how beautiful she looked; she was everything I wanted. But not like that. Not when she hadn't chosen to be with me, but had been told I was to be her partner.

She patted the bed next to her, inviting me to go and sit beside her. My legs trembled as I crossed the room; every step seemed to take forever. I sat down and took her hand. I wanted to say something to her about us, tell her I knew she didn't really want me, that she was only there because she had to. But I couldn't find the words; my brain seemed to have stopped.

She put her hand behind my head and pulled me towards her. She wanted me to kiss her. And I did. Her lips were soft but confident and they stopped the trembling in mine. I felt like I was melting and I thought, 'Maybe it's going to be alright.'

Then she pulled away. 'I'm going to the bathroom to get ready for bed. Do you want to get washed in here?'

I agreed, grateful for the washbasin in the corner; I could undress and be in bed before she came back. It would be less embarrassing that way.

By the time she came back, I *was* in bed, but I was also terrified again.

'Is that going to be your side then?'

I hadn't even thought of discussing it with her, I'd just climbed into the side nearest where I'd washed and undressed.

'Is that okay with you Jess?'

'Doesn't bother me at all.'

She climbed in beside me.

'Whoops, forgot to turn the light out.'

She moved like she was going to get out of bed again.

'Don't worry, I'll do it.'

I hurried over to the light switch and then blindly made my way back to the bed. The strangeness of the room and the dark made me lose my way and I banged my toe on the chair in the corner. I wanted to cry.

Back in bed she put her arms round my neck and kissed me again. Her body was soft against mine and her skin felt so smooth. I wanted to make love to her, but I couldn't. I kept thinking, 'It's not you she wants' and it made me feel helpless.

Jess didn't mind that I couldn't manage that night. Well, at least she said she didn't. She called it performance anxiety and said it happened to other men. As always she made me feel better.

# Twenty Four

For a lot of reasons life changed at The Larches after the wedding. For the members who hadn't married, the changes were all for the good; the pressure on accommodation had eased with the opening up of the attics and now there were five bathrooms so the morning congestion was much less frantic.

It wasn't as easy for the couples though. At first it was the difficulty of getting used to living so closely with a new partner. I found it especially hard. For years I'd fantasised about how it would be with Jess. In my most private moments I'd imagined holding her, kissing her, making love to her. I'd dreamt of telling her I loved her and her saying the same.

But it wasn't like that. She told me she loved me, but I couldn't believe her; it wasn't in her eyes, it wasn't in her touch. I felt she was acting a part, pretending to be my wife when all the time she wanted to be with Elijah. Sometimes I lay awake as she slept beside me, wondering how she really felt about the situation, wishing that I could wake her up and ask her. Even if I'd done that, I couldn't have believed whatever she said. Why would she tell me the truth when our lives were so wrapped up in pretence? But I wanted to know. Was she happy? How did she feel when she saw Elijah and Rebecca go into their room next door? What did she think when she heard the noises coming from their room night after night.

Night after night. It wasn't night after night in our room. It happened sometimes certainly, but not very often. Jess always made the first move and I would follow her lead. Even though I'd got over my performance anxiety, I still didn't dare face the possibility of rejection.

Still, I longed to talk to her about our relationship; not just about the sex, but about all of it. I couldn't though; if she'd told me she wasn't happy, that she longed to be with Elijah, I wouldn't have been able to live with myself. Our relationship was very fragile and I was so afraid of it shattering in pieces around me and how that would affect both us and the rest of The Community.

So for me, and I suspected for some of the other newly-weds, the pleasure of living at The Larches had dimmed. Outside our room we acted as though we were a 'real' couple, but when that door closed there was often a heavy silence that I could feel pressing down on me, making me feel trapped and uncomfortable.

There was something else worrying me. Sometimes I looked at the calendar to find out how long we had been together. One month, three months, five months and no sign of a baby. It didn't seem to be happening for the others either; I was quite glad about that. What if they had all made an announcement that they were expecting babies? How would that make me look? They'd know it was all my fault, that I was inadequate and not performing *my duties* as often as I should.

One evening Will stood up at the evening meal and cleared his throat. I had a panicky thought that he was going to announce Andrea's pregnancy, but it was just to say there wouldn't be a Circle Time that night.

But it couldn't be much longer before the announcement was made. What would I do then?

# Twenty Five

'Liam, will you be my Daddy instead of Elijah?'

'I can't do that, Becky, Mummy's married to Elijah. That makes him your Daddy.'

'But I don't like him.'

'Course you do. Only the other week you told me that you loved Elijah and you were glad he married Mummy.'

'Well I don't like him any more. He smacked me.'

That surprised me. Elijah had many faults, but I couldn't imagine him smacking a child, particularly Becky.

'What made him smack you?'

'I put orange jelly in his shoes.'

I imagined Elijah's face as he slid his foot into a shoe full of jelly and hid my smile.

'I think I might have smacked you too if you put jelly in my shoes. Yuk. What on earth made you do that?'

'I wanted to make him laugh. He's always so cross.'

That was something I'd noticed too. He was usually serious, but he'd always been willing to play and laugh with the children or chat with the adults. That didn't seem to be happening anymore and he was spending most of his time telling people off and pointing out their mistakes.

'Why did everybody have to get married anyway?'

'God wanted them to get married, sweetheart.'

'Tammy says it's so they can have babies. Is that true?'

'That's one reason, yes.'

'But Mummy doesn't need a baby. She's got me.'

'When Mummy and Elijah have a baby you'll still be their little girl. They'll still love you just as much.'

'Do you think so?'

'Of course they will.'

George had taken assembly, but Elijah asked if he could say a quick word before everyone went to dinner. George returned to his seat and Elijah took his place. He opened the Bible before he spoke.

'Thanks George for that. I want to read you something from Hebrews and then I'll explain the reason I'm adding to George's excellent assembly.

"Indeed, the word of God is living and active, sharper than any two-edged sword, piercing until it divides soul from spirit, joints from marrow; it is able to judge the thoughts and intentions of the heart." Hebrews four, verse twelve.

'Nothing could be more important than the word of God. Especially for us here in this religious community. But we aren't studying his word enough. We listen to it in assemblies. Sometimes we discuss it in Circle Time. But only on Sunday afternoons do we all study his word together. It's not enough—we need to do more.'

Elijah closed the Bible with a clap.

'From next week, we are going to make more space in our lives for God's word. Instead of Social Hour on Tuesdays and Thursdays, Circle Time will last from seven to nine. Those two hours will be spent in Bible study. No games, no chatting, just Bible discussion and study. The readings to be studied and discussed will be posted on the notice board on Monday and Wednesday evenings and you will be expected to be prepared for the discussion by Circle Time.'

In my heart I knew Elijah was right, we did need to spend more time studying the Bible. But it was surprising what a difference losing those two Social Hours made. We couldn't catch up on the news and I found that I quite often couldn't sleep on those nights because I hadn't relaxed enough from the work of the day.

The other difficulty was that sometimes people had to miss Monday or Wednesday Social Hours so that they could be prepared for the Bible Study Circle Times.

Still, Friday evenings became extra special.

*Friday evening, dinner time*

I pushed my chair back from the table, full and happy.

'Sausage and mash then treacle sponge with custard. That's good grub isn't it, Becky?'

Becky nodded. She couldn't speak; her mouth was too full of pudding. Jess laughed.

'Look at the two of you. I can't tell which one is the greediest.'

Becky swallowed loudly and giggled as she pointed to me

'He's greedy. I'm just hungry.'

I picked her up from her chair to tickle her before realising it wasn't such a good idea when she'd just eaten so much. I sat her on my knee instead until Elijah came up behind us.

'Come on, Becky. Let's go and wash that sticky face before Circle Time. Why are you such a messy girl?'

He grabbed her hand and pulled her away from me. She looked up as though she was asking for help, but I couldn't do anything for her.

*Circle Time*

George said, 'We've got a new game for tonight. Your Group Leader will give each one of you a sheet with ten sticky stars on it. I'm going to read out ten statements and I want you to stick a star on the back of someone who matches that statement. Some of them will be in your group; others will be out of everyone.'

The group leaders handed each group member a sheet of stars. Mine were yellow.

'OK, here we go.

1. In your group—someone you like praying with.
2. From everyone—someone wearing blue.
3. From everyone—someone who gives you comfort.
4. In your group—someone who knows a lot about the Bible.
5. From everyone—someone with brown shoes.
6. In your group—a friend.
7. From everyone—someone who makes you smile.
8. In your group—someone who works hard.
9. From everyone—someone you trust a lot.
10. From everyone—someone who shares your room.'


As George gave out the instructions, there was a lot of laughter and running about. I couldn't believe how many stars were put on my back—not just for my blue t-shirt either.

'Right! In your groups for the counting. Probably best if you split into pairs and count each other. Find who has the most stars in your group.'

I counted Will's stars, all thirty four of them. Then Will counted mine. I had sixty. It was the highest in my group—what a surprise.

'Can the ones with the highest number of stars in each group please come to the front.'

I went to the front with Gideon, Jess, Elijah and Ruth. George asked us to tell everyone how many stars we had.

Elijah, '58.'
Gideon, '50.'
Jess, '57.'

Me, '60.'

Ruth, '53.'

'Liam's the winner. And his prize is...'

I felt a little flutter in my chest, I didn't usually win things.

'A chance to read his favourite passage from the Bible.'

George gave me the Bible. It wasn't difficult to choose and I knew exactly where my passage was. I'd got used to reading in front of the others, although it had been really hard at first.

'Genesis two, verses seven to nine. "Then the LORD God formed man from the dust of the ground, and breathed into his nostrils the breath of life; and the man became a living being. ⁸And the LORD God planted a garden in Eden, in the east; and there he put the man whom he had formed. ⁹Out of the ground the LORD God made to grow every tree that is pleasant to the sight and good for food, the tree of life also in the midst of the garden, and the tree of the knowledge of good and evil."'

*Social Hour*

When I went into the Social Room it was absolute chaos. The children had decided they wanted an evening picnic so everyone was getting ready. Tom had found some old blankets to sit on; Liz had dug out plastic carrier bags, which she'd filled with biscuits, fruit and bottles of diluted squash. The children were running about, too excited to be careful, so both Josh and Paul were carrying their guitars protectively, trying to prevent them being damaged.

Eventually we were all ready to set off. Jonathan and Gideon led the way, through the kitchen garden, round the back of the house, down to the gatehouse and then back up the front path to the front lawn. On their journey they pretended to spot lions and tigers and warned everyone they must be very quiet so they wouldn't be attacked. Only Becky was fooled by this game and she held onto Elijah's hand so he could protect her.

When we reached the lawn we all spread out blankets and sat in little groups, munching on biscuits and drinking squash. The children raced from group to group grabbing biscuits as they ran.

It had been a hot day, but the air was cooler and more refreshing. When Paul and Josh began to play it made us want to sing, but as we relaxed and began to talk quietly the music became more subdued, a background cushion against which everyone could relax.

Jess and I mainly had a blanket to ourselves, although we were occasionally joined by Tammy and Becky. I lay on my side looking up at Jess.

'This is great.'

Jess sat hugging her knees. She looked around her.

'A good ending to the week. I think everyone was ready for a break.'

'I'm missing Tuesday and Thursday Social Hours, aren't you?'

Jess looked serious. 'Yes I am, but that's why we're here.'

We were interrupted by Becky who flung herself on the blanket between us.

'Tammy won't play with me any more. She says I'm cross because I'm tired, but I'm not tired, I'm not.'

Becky struggled to stop a yawn.

Jess lifted her arm. 'I know you're not tired, Becky, but I think you need a cuddle. Come here.'

Becky snuggled next to Jess and Jess put her arm round Becky's shoulders. She winked at me.

'Music's nice isn't it, Becky?'

'Mmm.'

Becky's thumb went in her mouth, a habit which usually got her in trouble with Elijah, but luckily he wasn't around.

I watched as Becky went to sleep leaning against Jess. I thought what a pretty picture they made. Jess should have children, that was for sure, she was a natural mother.

The sky gradually darkened. Someone went into the house and turned on the lights. Everyone began gathering up their blankets and the debris from the picnic. Jess picked up Becky to carry her into the house and I followed behind.

# Twenty Six

I saw Gideon running towards the greenhouse where I was working. He signalled for me to come out to him. As I walked towards him I realised he was very upset.

'Liam, Jess is crying and we don't know what to do. You've got to come and talk to her.'

He turned and began to walk quickly towards the house. I followed him.

'Why is she crying? Do you know?'

He looked at me and his lips trembled as if he was about to cry himself.

'Err... well... me and Jonathan; we were looking at this book...' His voice broke.

'Why is Jess crying about you looking at a book?'

He took a deep breath. 'No, it's not 'cos of that. Elijah came in and he was very angry when he saw what we were reading.'

I could only think of one reason why Elijah would be angry about the boys reading a book.

'Gideon, was it a *rude* book?'

He blushed and nodded. 'He said that books are one of the ways that Satan gets hold of innocent children like me and Jonathan. He says we've been tempted to sin.'

'So is that why Jess is crying?'

'Not really. Elijah says he's going to burn all the books in the library so we don't get tempted again.'

We'd reached the library by then and I could hear Jess sobbing. She was at one of the tables, her head in her hands. Tammy and Louise were standing either side of her stroking her hair and telling her not to cry. Becky was in a corner, sucking her thumb. Daniel and Jonathan were at another table, trying to pretend it wasn't happening.

Jonathan looked at Gideon. 'Does Liam know?'

Gideon nodded. I closed the door behind us and the noise made Jess look up.

'Has Gideon told you what Elijah said?'

'He says Elijah's planning to burn all the books.'

I looked around at the shelves of books. There were hundreds in there. Paul had told me that some of them were quite valuable—first editions or something. I didn't know anything about first editions, but I did know that the books were very important to Jess.

She took hold of my hand. 'How can he burn all this? What can we do to stop him?'

She looked up at me pleadingly. The children too were staring hopefully at me. For most of my life I'd stood back and let things happen, but I couldn't do that now. This was a time to fight against something which was obviously wrong. Jess might not be in love with me, but she seemed to feel that I could help.

I took a deep breath. 'How's about we go to talk to him? Me and you. Maybe we could persuade him.'

She tried to smile and almost managed. 'It's worth a try.'

'Okay, go and wash your face and then we'll go and talk to him.'

She left the room and I tried to calm my breathing, which had speeded up to match the rapid beating of my heart. The children kept on looking at me.

'Right, kids, let's find you something to do while Jess is gone. Err...' I stopped to think a minute. 'I know, why don't you write a letter to Elijah about why we need to keep the books? They might come in useful if this doesn't work.'

Jonathan found them some paper and gave each one a piece.

'I don't know what to write.' Tammy said.

'Okay,' said Jonathan, 'Let's get together some ideas and I'll write them on the board.'

'Can you manage, Jonathan?'

'Course I can, you go and wait for Jess.'

As I closed the door behind me I noticed that my hands were wet. I was wiping them on my jeans when Jess turned up. She took my, thankfully now dry, hand.

'I'm glad you're here to help, Liam.'

That was just what I needed to help stop my hands shaking.

'Come on, Jess, let's go and see what we can do.'

Luckily Paul was in the office with Elijah so there were three of us to persuade him. He was very angry at first. He said we had no right to question his decisions, that he was responsible for the moral welfare of the whole community and, as far as he was concerned, the only book we needed was the Bible. It was a story book, a spiritual guide and a history book. What more did we need?

Paul was the first to try to persuade him otherwise. 'How can Jess teach young children to read if they only have the Bible? The language is very complicated.'

'Jess is perfectly capable of simplifying extracts for them. Most of the books in the library have language as complex as the Bible. You're arguing against yourself there, Paul.'

Elijah sat back in his chair with a smug smile.

I had an idea. 'How can our children learn about the world we have to save if they don't learn anything about it? They'll grow up thinking that everywhere is the same as here. They have to understand the enemy before they can fight against them.'

That made Jess speak up; she'd been quiet until then.

'That's right, Elijah. We have a duty to teach these children about the world.'

Elijah nodded as if he were thinking about what she'd said and I was more confident now we'd got his attention. 'How would it be if Jess made a list of the books she thinks are suitable?'

'I'd be happy to do that, Elijah. You wouldn't need to take my word for it; others could look through the list to check it.'

Elijah was quiet for a minute and then he said, 'You can do your list. Get Paul, Rachel and George to look at it with you then give it to me. I have the final word though.'


We all helped with teaching the children whilst Jess did the list. It took a week. Then it was another week before it had been checked by everybody. Elijah crossed off some of the chosen ones, but we were left with about fifty books from the original four hundred and eight. I hadn't heard of a lot of the ones we were going to keep, but Jess told me they were classics.

The bonfire had been arranged for a Saturday evening. There was a special assembly beforehand and then we went out into the garden. Ian had got a small bonfire going.

Elijah said we should take turns at throwing the books on. The children were very excited, they danced around the fire and sang, 'Another one gone, another one gone!' I don't think they truly understood what they were doing. Elijah was excited too, he couldn't stand still, but strode around, laughing and shouting. He seemed to be everywhere all at once and he certainly went out of turn a few times to throw books on.

I didn't want to be involved, but Elijah handed a book to me saying, 'Come on, Liam.' To my shame I did as I was told, throwing the book into the flames and watching as the cover gradually shrivelled to nothing and the pages curled, scorching at the edges and then dissolving into ashes. I hated myself. I felt dirty, taking part in something which was very wrong and yet I was powerless to stop. I hid at the back of the crowd and hoped that Elijah wouldn't make me do it again.

Jess didn't throw any books on the fire. She hadn't wanted to be there at all, but Elijah insisted. He said she'd be setting a bad example to the children if she didn't go. She tried to keep them from seeing she was crying all the time we were out there.

A lot of the other adults seemed to be feeling bad too. They were very quiet and, although Liz had put potatoes in the fire to bake, many said they were tired and wanted an early night.

When I went up to our room Jess was sitting on the windowsill, gazing up at the stars. She turned when I opened the door.

'Liam, that was so horrible!'

I hurried to put my arms round her and pulled her towards me. I stroked her back and said, 'I know, I know.'

She started to sob. I pulled her over to the bed and sat her on my knee, holding on to her until she seemed to calm a little. I put my hand under her chin and lifted her face until she was looking directly into my eyes.

'He didn't get to burn all of them,' I said.

A tear ran down her left cheek and fell on to her t-shirt. 'No, not all of them. Just most of them. How could he do that?'

I ran my finger over her cheek, trying to dry it. 'Sometimes Elijah does things we can't understand but we have to accept what he does because he's our leader.'

Jess took hold of my hand and twisted her fingers into mine. She turned her gaze away and looked down at our locked hands.

'I've been... been, err, thinking about leaving.'

I couldn't believe it. 'What would you do? Where would you go?'

The question, 'What about me?' stayed in my head. I didn't have the courage to ask that question; I couldn't bear to hear the answer.

'I don't know what I'd do or where I'd go. I've dedicated my life to this place and to Elijah, now I feel I've lost everything.'

She put her head on my shoulder so her soft hair was against my neck. She was quiet for a while and then she began to talk in a voice that I struggled to hear.

'I loved Elijah. Did you know that?'

'I did know that'

'I would have done anything for him. I've done things for him that I'm ashamed of. I've told lies. I've manipulated people. I've passed on secrets that I'd promised never to tell.'

I couldn't believe it. 'Jess, you would never do anything wrong. I know that. You've such an honest person.'

'But you don't know everything about me. Remember that day when you tried to leave and I met you and persuaded you to stay? Elijah had been watching you and he knew you were unhappy. He saw you hide the wheelbarrow and set off to the back of the house. He sent me out to talk to you. He knew you liked me.'

'But he told you off in front of everybody and stopped you being Day Leader. Why would he do that? What was in it for him?'

'He saw the flower growing business as the natural way for us to go, but he needed someone with experience. Paul had been talking to someone in the town centre when you went past one day. You were drunk. This man told Paul how good a gardener you had been before your boss, Harry, died. Paul had mentioned this to Elijah and he'd suggested we give you the chance to

141

come here to recover. Elijah persuaded me it was a good idea. I feel guilty about it now, but then it all seemed so natural just to follow whatever he said.'

I couldn't speak. It was such a shock. Jess stroked my hair back off my face and looked into my eyes again.

'Liam, are you okay.'

I shook my head. I was so full of feelings, but I couldn't work out what they were. Pain, anger, shock. But underneath it all was the thought that Elijah had wanted me, needed me so much he'd made Jess lie and humiliated her in front of everyone just to keep me there.

Jess stood up. 'Come on, let's go to bed.' I didn't know what else to do so I agreed. We undressed and climbed into bed, but we couldn't sleep, just held each other for comfort.

When the light was off it was my turn to talk. I had to tell her how I felt.

'Jess, I love you. I've loved you ever since we worked together in the garden.'

'All that time? You never said anything to me. Why didn't you say anything?'

'I'm not good enough for you. I never will be.'

'You are good enough for me, Liam. You're a wonderful person. But I thought we were just friends. You never gave any sign at all.'

'There was something else. I thought you were *with* Elijah.'

'What made you think I was with Elijah?'

'I saw you… together.'

'When? How? I don't understand.'

'You were in one of the bedrooms. It was the day we celebrated the kitchen extension.' In the darkness I could feel my face going red. 'You were…' I couldn't go on.

'I was what?'

'You knelt in front of him and undid his belt.'

142

Jess sat up in bed. 'Oh my God. I remember that day. We just didn't think about what we were doing until afterwards. You saw us? You saw me and Elijah? I can't believe it.'

'I ran away. No one ever knew because it seemed worse out there so I came back. I came back to be with you, just to live in the same place, to make sure you were safe and happy. I never expected us to end up married, especially after...'

'Oh no, Liam, is there something else?'

'That day when Elijah sent me down the cellar and you brought me back up. I heard you say to him that you didn't want me.'

'I've hurt you so much and yet you still love me. I can't believe it.'

'You didn't hurt me on purpose. Just tell me; was there something between you and Elijah?'

'Elijah always had some sort of hold over me. We had a sexual relationship at university and it just seemed to carry on when I met him again. But I never expected any commitment from him. I knew he also went with Rebecca and Gemma, maybe even some of the others. I think we all felt it was some kind of honour.'

I was scared now and had to ask another question. 'Has it happened since we married?'

'No. Oh no. He even said to me he had realised that what he had been doing was wrong. He vowed he wouldn't go with other women after he married Rebecca and I believe him. She was always the one he wanted most. I wouldn't be unfaithful to you either.'

'I'm glad.'

We stopped talking then. It was a lot to take in. I suppose we must have drifted off to sleep, but as soon as the sun rose we woke again.

I put my arm around her and pulled her towards me.

'Are you still thinking of leaving?'

'I don't know what else to do.'

'If you go, can I come with you?'

'Of course. I wouldn't leave you behind. Not after all we've been through. You're very special to me and the only one I ever want to be with.'

For the next hour or so we went over and over it. How practical leaving was. Whether we could start again somewhere else. If we could leave all the people we were close to—Becky and the other children, Rebecca, Josh, Will, Tom…

We came to a decision. We would stay. Make the best of it. Be there to stand up to Elijah if he ever went too far.

Later Jess told me that was the night she began to truly love me. We'd been open with each other and forgiven what there was to forgive so we could start again. And once we two became one we were stronger for the difficulties that were to follow.

# Twenty Seven

Early Sunday morning. The sun pushed a finger of light through a gap in the curtains to touch the single pink rose, a gift from me to Jess, in a drinking glass on the bedside table.

I opened my eyes and looked at the ceiling before turning on my side to look at Jess sleeping peacefully beside me. I propped myself up on my elbow to get a better view.

Jess was lying at a slight angle towards me, her hair spread across the pillow. I sighed happily; feeling so lucky that we were together. I loved everything about her. The smell of her hair. The silky feel of her skin. The plump firmness of her breasts. The roundness of her belly. I nestled in the sound of her soft breathing, basked in the warmth of her body.

Unthinking, I reached out a hand and gently stroked her check. She stirred and opened one eye to look at me.

'Time is it?'

I picked my watch up from the bedside cabinet and smiled.

'Early.'

She turned on to her side to face me more directly.

'How early?'

'Very early.'

She smiled and slid her body closer to mine.

'Good.'

She reached out a hand and hooked one finger under my chin to draw me even closer to her.

It was another Sunday morning a couple of months later when I woke to the sound of the bedroom door closing. I had a fairly good idea where Jess was going and, when she came back in, her pale face showed me I was right.

'Have you been sick again?'

'Yes. Looks like I might be having a baby. Either that or I have a terrible stomach bug.'

She took hold of the covers to climb back into bed. I lifted my arm, inviting her to cuddle up against my chest, but she shook her head.

'Sorry, think I might need to go again in a minute.'

'How are we going to find out?'

'Elijah's not going to let me go to the doctor is he?'

I put on my serious Elijah face. 'We don't need doctors in this community for we know we can take our sickness to Jesus and he will heal us.'

Elijah didn't trust doctors at all, he said they put themselves above God because they made life and death decisions, which only He could take. He'd forbidden everyone in The Community from having anything to do with doctors.

'But I'm not sick, am I?'

I smiled.

'Alright, clever clogs, I *have been* sick this morning, but that's almost definitely because I'm having a baby, not because I'm ill. How are we ever going to find out for sure if I can't see a doctor?'

'What about one of those pregnancy test things? Where do you get one from?'

'They sell them at chemists, a place we never go to and they cost money, which we haven't got. Could you use some float money and go when you're on your rounds?'

'George has eyes like a hawk, he watches every penny. I'd need to get permission first, sign for the money, bring back receipts and sign again. I couldn't just sneak it past him.'

'Well, you'll have to ask him then. Tell him what we want and why we want it. He won't mind.'

'What if he says something or laughs at me. It's embarrassing. Can't you ask him, Jess, please?'

'It's no good me asking for it. The person who's going to spend the money has to sign for it and George knows I don't go into town. It has to be you.'

I'd known all along I'd have to ask for it, I was just looking for some sort of loophole that would get me out of it. I took a deep breath and went straightaway so I didn't worry about it any more.


'George, I was wondering if I could have some money for Monday.'

'Money? What do you want money for? Isn't your float enough?'

'It's not that. I need to buy something.'

'Liam, Liam, Liam. What could you possibly want that we don't have here? Look around. You have a nice home and the best family in the world. You have the Lord above to care for you. You're well fed and well dressed...' he looked me up and down, taking in the hole in the knee of my jeans and the button missing on my shirt, '...well, reasonably dressed. What more could you need?'

This was turning out even more difficult than I'd expected. I swallowed hard.

'We, ere, think... Jess... could be, erm, pregnant and we need a pregnancy test kit to find out for sure.'

Then he started laughing and I started blushing. He was laughing at me. And Jess. Then the embarrassment started to wear off and I began to feel angry. How dare he laugh at us like that? We were married, we hadn't done anything wrong. He must have seen the look on my face.

147

'Oh, Liam, I'm so sorry. I'm not laughing at you. It just seems so funny because, only this morning, Will asked me that same question. They think that Andrea is pregnant too. I said I'd see what I could sort out.'

I relaxed. It sounded like Will and Andrea were going through the same sort of worries as me and Jess. George spoke again.

'Tell you what. It's probable this is going to happen again with the other couples. Why don't you buy five pregnancy test kits so we're ready for when it happens again?'

Here was another embarrassment. It just got worse Buy five kits. Five! George gave me a handful of notes— neither of us knew how much the kits would be. I signed for the money and went off to spend a sleepless night worrying about having to walk into a chemist and ask for five kits. They'd think I was some sort of weirdo.

It took a while but I eventually found a way round it. There were two biggish chemists and one small one on my route. The two bigger ones were likely to have these kits on the shelf so I wouldn't have to ask to buy them. I could buy two at each of those. Then I'd get one at the other chemist. I had it all sorted.

The first one I called at was 'Harvey's Chemist.' It was a big place and I spent a few minutes wandering round trying to find the kits. They weren't out on open shelves, but they were on the counter where I could pick two up and hand them to the assistant.

After a few minutes looking at combs, trying to pluck up courage, I walked slowly to the counter. I know it was stupid, but my heart was beating really fast—I was convinced that everyone was looking at me and they'd know, just know what I was doing. The kits were slightly to the back and I leant over to pick two up. I didn't look at the labels or anything but I knew they were the right thing. What I didn't know was that they were different brands.

'Eight pounds for the Easy Test and seven pounds fifty for B Sure. Is that alright?'

She had a very loud voice. I nodded, hoping it would be enough to shut her up.

'They'll both give the same result you know. No need to go for different brands to make sure.'

'One's for a friend,' I whispered.

She cupped her hand to her ear.

'Sorry, I'm a bit deaf today. What did you say?'

I could feel the whole world looking at me.

'I said it's for a friend,' in my slightly quieter than normal voice.

'Oh right. Did your friend ask for a specific brand?' she shouted.

'No, no, I just wanted to get two.'

'Well, let's see if we can find which one's best.' She looked round the shop. 'Liz,' she yelled, 'Liz!'

Liz turned round.

She waved the tests in the air.

'Do you know which one of these is best?'

Liz opened her mouth to speak, but then looked behind my assistant and turned away, pretending to do something else. A big red-faced man had his hand on my assistant's shoulder. He had a deep booming voice.

'What's going on here, Margaret? Why are you yelling across the shop floor like that?'

Everyone froze so they could watch what was happening. Margaret looked embarrassed but not as embarrassed as I was.

'Well, this man here wanted to buy two test kits and I was trying to find out which was the best. I thought Liz would know.'

'I think I've told you before that the customer is always right. If he wants to buy two different test kits that's his decision not yours.'

'But he wasn't bothered what brand it was.'

'Did he ask for your opinion?'

'He said he hadn't realised …'

'Did he ask for your opinion?' His voice was like threatening thunder.

'No.'

'So he was happy with his choice?'

She seemed to have become smaller somehow. 'Yes.'

He turned to me.

'Now, sir, did you choose these two kits?'

'I just picked them up.'

'And are you happy with them?'

I couldn't have made a decision even if I wanted to. 'Yes.'

'Did you hear that, Margaret? He's happy with these two kits. There's absolutely no need for you to go shouting round the shop about 'best' is there?'

'No.' Her eyes were watery, as if she were about to cry.

'We'll talk some more about this in a minute. I'll finish up here and you go in the back to wait for me.' He watched her go then turned and shook his head at me.

'Sorry about that, sir. We just can't get the staff these days. Now let's wrap these up.'

He rang the two kits into the till, took my money, slid the two boxes into a bag and handed it to me. I ran from the shop, my skin burning and almost ready to cry myself.

That was my last attempt to buy two kits at a time. I asked my customers and found other chemists so I could just buy one kit at a time. When I got back George laughed because I had four different receipts, but he didn't understand how embarrassing the whole thing was.

*

Jess had wanted me to be with her whilst she did the test, but we couldn't work out how to get us both in the bathroom at the same time—goodness knows what anyone would think if they saw us. We decided it was best for her to do it on her own. The morning after my shopping trip she jumped out of bed very early, grabbed the kit and raced into the bathroom. It seemed hours till she came back. When she did, she looked happy, but very pale. It turned out that the test had been positive, but all that rushing about early in the morning had made her sick. I hugged her briefly before she had to dash back into the bathroom again.

It was noisy as usual as everyone ate dinner and chatted about their day. We stood up nervously and I coughed to make everyone quiet. It didn't quite work, some people were still talking. Jess held my hand as I took a deep breath. The words came out louder than I'd intended.

'We've got an announcement to make.'

That made them quiet. The people with their backs to us turned our way. I could feel the blush spreading over my body and up into my face. Jess squeezed my hand to encourage me to carry on. She was happy to speak, but I was determined to do it.

'We're having a baby.'

There was a loud cheer and lots of clapping. Everyone looked so happy. Apart from Elijah who was looking down at the table, his face frozen. I was distracted by a movement further along the table. It was Will and Andrea standing up.

'We were going to make the same announcement. Trust these two to beat us to it!'

The cheer was even louder and then everyone began to talk to each other about the excitement of two babies being due. It was like we didn't exist, the babies were the important ones. Jess and I looked at Will and Andrea; we all shrugged and sat down. My cheeks were burning, I had tears in my eyes and I knew I couldn't possibly eat anything more so I just gazed at Jess, dreaming of holding our baby in my arms. Elijah brushed past me as he left the dining room. It seemed he wasn't in the mood to celebrate.

Jess was getting fatter and fatter. When I snuggled up to her at night, I could feel her tummy moving under my hand. She complained the baby was keeping her awake by doing that, but I loved knowing that was our baby moving around.

It was unbelievable: Ruth and Gemma announced their pregnancies within the next two months. There were lots of jokes about something in the water; Elijah and Rebecca never laughed along with everyone else. The four pregnant women called themselves the Cradle Club and huddled in corners comparing symptoms.

I used to talk to the baby a lot, lying with my head on Jess's stomach and telling the baby all about when I was younger and looked after Steven and the twins. I was sure the baby could hear because it stopped moving to listen. I couldn't wait until it was born and I could hold it in my arms and talk properly. And find out if it was a boy or a girl.

Jess seemed to worry a lot more than she used to. She really wanted to see a doctor, but Elijah had said again and again that childbirth was a natural process and we didn't need medical help as we had God watching over us. I knew all that was true, but we both wished she could be checked over just to make sure. And we had a question we wanted to ask. Should we make love? Would that hurt the baby? We worried about that and said we wouldn't, but sometimes it just seemed to happen. I loved Jess so much, but I loved the baby too. I was very gentle with Jess and prayed that it wouldn't do any harm. Jess kept saying she'd talk it over with the Cradle Club, but then she didn't like to bring it up, it was too embarrassing.

She had another worry too. A letter arrived from the Education Authority, saying they were coming to inspect the school in a month's time. I kept saying there was no need to worry because she was so good at teaching, but she had the idea that if anything went wrong they'd bring the social workers in and take the children away. She couldn't bear the thought of that and neither could I; I knew what foster care could do to a child.

We were looking for ideas of something special to do. Jess had been thinking of doing a play for an Afternoon Assembly; I don't know what reminded me, but I mentioned that time when the children made a Noah's Ark and wondered whether that would do. She thought that was a good idea so she asked Paul to write a script. The visitors would see a rehearsal. She was also going to do a lot of display work and maybe show them a maths lesson. It would be a lot of extra work for her and I hoped she didn't do too much and make herself ill.

Elijah didn't want those people coming to look at our school. He said they had no right to come and look around. Jess told me he had a point, but she was so afraid of them bringing in Social Services, she wanted to do what they asked.

Elijah wasn't keen on anything around that time. He was very bad tempered and just wanted us to work and pray, not take any time for ourselves. If he saw the Cradle Club he shouted at the women and asked if they had no work to do. I hoped that Rebecca became pregnant soon so that, perhaps, he'd relax a bit.

# Twenty Eight

On the day of the inspection, Jess got up with me at five. She hadn't slept well and she didn't see any point in lying in bed and looking at the ceiling for another couple of hours.

While I went off to get my deliveries ready, she went into the library. One of the things she'd realised during the night was that all those empty shelves would look bad to the inspectors so she was going to find some of the children's craft work and put it on display. She was also going to use the space to put some of the workbooks and papers out too.

It was a lovely spring day and I worked happily for a couple of hours until it was time to eat. I arrived at the dining room just as Jess was going in.

'Come and look what I've done.'

'Oh, Jess, I'm hungry. Can't it wait?' I smiled as I said it, in the hope she'd know I was joking.

'No jokes this morning, I left my sense of humour in bed.'

She opened the library door and said, 'Ta da!'

'Oh, Jess, it's brilliant. They can't fail to be impressed.'

It did look better, but I have to say it still looked quite empty. Obviously she hadn't been able to put anything on the top shelves, she hadn't enough stuff and she couldn't reach.

'Wait, I've had an idea. Let's get some plants and put them on some of the higher shelves. I've potted some up ready to take out to the shops, but they can wait until tomorrow.'

'Oh, that's great. I was worried about the higher shelves.'

When the plants were arranged, they really seemed to fill a lot of the space and we were both pleased with the result.

On our way to the dining room, we met Paul.

'Have you seen Elijah?'

'Not since last night.'

'Hope he turns up soon, we've got an important business meeting this morning.'

Back in the dining room, we helped ourselves to a cooked breakfast but when Jess put the first forkful towards her mouth, her face changed.

'Oh, no, not today,' she managed to say before having to dash from the room.

She didn't return and the next time I saw her she was sitting on the steps outside.

'Just getting some fresh air.'

'I'm off to do my deliveries.'

'I'm scared, there's so much riding on this.'

'Don't worry, it will be fine. They're good kids with a good teacher, what could they not like about that?'

She squeezed my hand. 'Thanks for that.'

When I got back to The Larches after my deliveries Josh was just telling the inspectors where to park their cars. I knew I couldn't do anything to help so I went off to do the million and one jobs that I was always trying to find time for. I got so involved that I almost missed lunchtime; when I realised I hurried off to grab what crumbs were left and to see if the inspectors had gone.

The inspectors had obviously left because the children were out on the lawn. There were also the remains of a picnic on a chequered tablecloth, but they must have eaten their fill because they were busy turning cartwheels at the far end of the lawn. Only Becky wasn't with them. She was on her own and I didn't need to ask why. She hadn't yet mastered cartwheels and she liked to practise on her own. As soon as she saw me, she came running over.

She was breathless when she spoke. 'Hello, Liam, did you see me? I nearly did it that I time.'

'I did. Brilliant. How did the inspection go?'

'Think it was okay. They didn't shout or anything and Jess was smiling when she said goodbye.'

'Where is Jess?'

'She's gone upstairs. Mummy's not feeling very well so she's gone to check on her.'

'Not well? What's wrong?'

'Don't know, but Jess said I haven't to worry so I'm not. Mummy just needs to take it easy.'

'Alright, Becks, you carry on with your practice and I'll see you later.'

I grabbed a sandwich; it was a bit curly but it saved me having to go into the kitchen and beg from Liz. I wanted to see Jess as soon as possible so I didn't want to waste time. I ran up the stairs to the attic landing where I could hear voices in Rebecca and Elijah's room. I knocked on the door and the voices stopped. The door opened a crack and Jess peered out. When she saw it was me, she slipped through the gap and closed the door behind her.

'I've been seeing to Rebecca.'

'What's wrong?'

'Her and Elijah have had a big argument and she's very upset about it.'

'They're always arguing; what's different about this one?'

'She won't tell me. There's definitely something wrong there, though.'

'Where's Elijah.'

'No one knows but you haven't to say anything about this to him. Promise?'

'I promise.'

'He's certainly been angry lately. Has Rebecca given you any clues what it's about?'

'She hasn't told me anything, but I suspect it's because she's not pregnant yet. I know she's worried about it and she has said that, as she's had a child already, it's probably not her. Maybe Elijah is worried he's infertile.'

'Should we talk to him? Maybe help him find a way to get rid of his anger.'

'Liam Donnelly, what did I say?'

'Oh, alright, I won't. But I don't think it's something to get so worried about.'

'Different things worry different people. Anyway, didn't you worry when I didn't get pregnant right away?'

I didn't think she'd noticed. 'You're right, I suppose?'

'I think Rebecca's ready for a nap. I'll just check and then I'll come downstairs for some lunch.'

'It's a bit late; there's probably nothing left. I grabbed a curly sandwich from the children's picnic. Oh, how did the inspection go?'

'Not bad. Tammy forgot her words and Becky splashed paint over everywhere, but apart from that...'

'Good. See you downstairs.'

# Twenty Nine

As that day went on, it became stranger and stranger.

We were out on the lawn with the children. They were playing Gospel Chase, a game invented by Gideon which had rules so complicated no adult had ever been able to work it out; Becky seemed to understand it perfectly. She rushed between us, shouting, 'Matthew, Mark, Luke and John,' then she clung to the back of Jess's legs as Tammie tried to pull her back towards the others. We heard the sound of a car coming up the drive and everyone turned to look.

Andrea was driving and there was someone in the back. She parked in front of the house, climbed out, went round to the back door and opened it. She reached in, took someone's arm and helped him out. George followed and took his other arm. The pair supported the man and led him into the house. As they reached the door, George signalled to me and Jess for us to come in.

It took a couple of minutes for my eyes to get used to the darkness of the hallway but then I saw the stranger push away from Andrea to stand in the middle of the hall, swaying slightly. He was an oldish man whose hair looked like it hadn't been combed for weeks. His once white t shirt was now grey and torn and his baggy old training pants were ripped and stained. The sole flapped on one shoe as he walked. He lifted his arms, increasing the various odours which filled the air, and then began to shout.

'Come on then, come and convert me. My soul needs saving!'

As the man windmilled his arms, someone pushed against my back and I heard a voice say, 'Pooh, what's that smell?' I turned round and gently pushed Becky outside. Then I went back into the hallway.

'D'you hear me? I'm waiting. Come and get me. I'm the heathen that needs retrievin'.'

The man brought his fists in to beat his chest making his voice vibrate in a wordless roar. Then he stood perfectly still.

'Oh wait, it's working.' He began to sing. 'Onward Christian Soldiers, marching as to war.'

I stepped forward, but Andrea shook her head and gently took the man's hand.

'With the cross of Jesus …'

'Come on, let's go and get you a drink.'

'Drink? What sort of drink? Whiskey?'

'No, not whiskey.'

'Gin, then. I want gin. Gin, gin, gin. It was the gin what did him in.'

'We don't have any gin. This is a place of God.'

I knew this man… but how?

'A church? A church? Have you got any wine? Come on, it's communion time. Communion party time. Get me a glass.'

He pointed towards the Assembly Room. 'Is the wine in there?'

'We don't have any wine, Joe. What about a cup of tea?'

Joe! Now I knew who it was.

'Alright, sweetheart. If you wanna make me a brew that's fine with me.'

I watched as my father smiled up at Andrea, his agitation calmed by her soothing voice. I, on the other hand, was feeling very agitated. I wanted to go and scream in his face, or tear him to pieces, or knock him to the floor and leave him there to die. But I stayed where I was, my heart burning and my body made of ice.

Andrea led Joe off into the dining room by the hand and the others left. All except me. I was surrounded by snatches of *Onward Christian Soldiers* and the familiar voice was holding me captive. Then I heard Jess and the children outside giving thanks for the success of the day. They ended with the Lord's Prayer and when I heard, 'And forgive us our trespasses, as we forgive those who trespass against us,' I knew it was time for me to go upstairs and do some thinking.

I couldn't bring myself to talk to Dad nor tell Jess about him. I tried to go on as normal, although, to be honest, things weren't really that normal. Elijah still hadn't turned up and everyone who knew about his disappearance was very worried about him. Jess presumed, at first, that I was acting strangely because of Elijah. She talked to me when we went to bed that night.

'Liam, do you know something about Elijah's disappearance that you're not telling us?'

'What makes you say that?'

'Well, you seem so distracted and, I don't know, worried. You haven't …' she took a deep breath, '*done* anything, have you? To Elijah?'

'No. Course not! How could you think that?'

'Well, I know you don't like him and I just thought …'

'No. There is something wrong but it's nothing to do with Elijah.'

'Well, what is it then?' Her voice rose, she was obviously imagining all sorts of things.

'You know that new man, Joe?'

'The one that Andrea picked up? I've seen him around but I haven't talked to him. Why?'

'He's my Dad.'

'Don't be silly! You're imagining things. You haven't seen him since you were eight.'

160

'It might be a long time since I saw him, but I know who he is. His voice is exactly the same. And his eyes. Have a look at them. They're my eyes.'

Silence. Jess shook her head, as if trying to clear the idea from her mind. Then she looked into my face and must have realised that it was definitely true.

'What are you going to do?'

'I don't know. I keep going over and over it, thinking about what happened that night. And what happened before that. They didn't have an easy life, either of them; all those children and no money. In that tiny little house. Maybe that's why he drank.'

'Are you saying you forgive him?'

'It's up to God to forgive him, isn't it? But am I a good enough Christian to take this man back into my life and leave it to God to make a judgement as to whether his time in prison made him repent?'

'You're a good Christian, Liam. No one could argue with that. But you're also a human being who had to deal with the most horrible thing at a very early age. No one could blame you for finding it difficult to deal with him. But I do think you should let him know who you are at least.'

'You're right. I know you're right. As usual!' I smiled at her. 'Are you going to tell me what to say?'

'No, that's up to you.'

'How did I know you were going to say that?' I put one hand on her shoulder and the other on her tummy where our baby was moving restlessly.

'Don't worry, you'll work it out.'

# Thirty

When Elijah hadn't come back the next day, George and Paul became really worried. They got Ruth to ring the hospitals and asked me to help them search the grounds. Most of The Community believed he was praying in private so they didn't realise there was anything to worry about.

We split up and began to look through the bushes and overgrown areas. Our cover story was that Methuselah had gone missing; Paul had locked him in the barn so no-one could suddenly discover him and stop us searching.

We had no joy searching the grounds and George decided we should look through the cellars. All the work had been done by this point and it would be my first time down there. Paul, at our request, went off to Elijah's office to find the key; he knew where it was kept.

George and I sat on the steps while we waited for him to come back.

George said, 'I've been worried about Elijah for a while. He's seemed so angry, especially at me. Do you know what it's about?'

I shook my head, 'No idea.'

'It's all a mystery to me. He and Rebecca had seemed so happy at first, now they barely speak. Rebecca doesn't seem to look after Becky as well as she used to and, as for Elijah, he's often downright cruel to poor Becky. I hope this all sorts itself out soon before Becky gets hurt anymore.'

Paul came bustling down the stairs. 'It's not there. We're not going to be able to get in.'

George opened his mouth to speak then closed it again.

'What is it?' Paul asked.

'I know I shouldn't have, but I had a spare one made. I kept thinking that things might go wrong. I'll go and get it.'

Then I was on my own with Paul. Another awkward conversation.

'I think Elijah might be heading for a breakdown,' Paul said, 'he's had one before.'

That was a surprise.

'What did you do last time?'

'We got him to the hospital, but there's no way he's going to agree with that this time. Not the way he feels about hospitals.'

George was back. With his spare key. He opened the door. There were the new stairs and then another, locked, door at the bottom. It worked with the same key. The first room was the kitchen. Down one wall, there was a sink, a fridge, a microwave and some kitchen units. The other three walls were lined with shelves full of tins and packets. The next room was some sort of bedroom, a long room filled from wall to wall with mattresses. Then there was a room that looked like an Assembly room and another containing the old sofas from the Social Room; we'd replaced them very recently. The doors stood open to a small bathroom and a separate toilet. The other toilet at the end of the corridor had its door closed. Paul went to try it. It was locked.

He tapped on the door. 'Elijah, are you in there?'

'Leave me alone,' a muffled voice said.

'Come on, Elijah, everyone's worried.'

'I'm alright. Go away.'

'Please, Elijah, just come out and talk to us. Don't make us force the door open.'

Silence for a minute; then Elijah fumbled with the lock and stepped outside. He was a mess. His clothes were filthy, his hair was matted and he had a scratch down his cheek. He looked towards George and I and pointed his finger.

'Get those two out of here.'

'They just want to help.'

'I don't care, get them away from me.'

Paul nodded and we went back upstairs. George was careful to retrieve his key from the door.

'You never know when these things come in handy.'

# Thirty One

Joe was now sober and seemed to be enjoying the rare luxury of regular meals, being looked after and sleeping in a comfortable bed. But that didn't mean he fitted in with The Community. One day, when I got back from my deliveries, I found Andrea and George in the office, talking about him. He had refused to get up for Morning Assembly and was now in the Social Room complaining very loudly that he was being kept prisoner.

'Do you want me to talk to him?'

'That's an unusual offer coming from you, Liam. You usually run a mile when it's anything like this.'

'Just thought I'd like to get more involved in that side of things, if that's alright with you?'

'Okay, but do you want me to come with you?'

'No thanks, Andrea. If I'm struggling I'll come and ask for help.'

I took a deep breath before I went into the Social Room where Joe was pacing the floor.

'Have you got the key then? Are you gonna let me out the front door?'

'Thought we might talk a bit first.' I was feeling decidedly uncomfortable.

'Oh my God, here we go again, another bloody sermon.' Joe threw himself backwards on to a chair and folded his arms. 'Get on with it then.'

'Do you remember me from a long time ago?'

Joe peered into my face. 'You do look a bit familiar. What's your name?

'It's Liam.' My heartbeat filled my ears. 'Liam Donnelly.' I wasn't sure I'd be able to hear his reply and, as a few minutes passed in silence, I was worried I'd missed it. Then he spoke in a very quiet voice and I had to strain to hear him.

'Our Liam? My eldest?

'That's right, Dad.'

'Eh, lad, I haven't seen you since the night of that terrible accident when your mum died.'

'It wasn't an accident. We both know that. I was there… remember?'

'It *were* an accident. Alright, I shouldn't have hit her but she provoked me. It was as much her fault as mine, but I'm the one who paid the price, spent eight years in prison when all I did was give her what she deserved.'

I held onto the arms of my chair. 'How can you say that? Have you learnt nothing since then?'

'You always were on her side, weren't you? Running here and there trying to do all the things she should have done. I did my best for all of you, but what could I do when she were such a terrible mother. You kids didn't stand a chance with her around.'

'You were the one who drank all the money away. You were the one who beat her black and blue when you'd been drinking, and us too if you had any energy left when you'd finished with her.' My voice became louder. 'You were the one who left an eight year old child,' I banged my fist against the coffee table, '*eight years old*, alone with his dying mother!'

I was crying now but I could see from my father's face that my words weren't having any effect. I took a deep breath to calm myself and spoke again.

'At the end of the day, it doesn't matter what I say to you, Dad. It's not me who's your judge. The Lord will judge you when the time comes. Until then, I'll pray for your soul because, no matter what you've done, you'll always be the man who's my earthly father. I forgive you, Dad, for what you did to our family because now I can see that you're a weak man who didn't have the strength to fight his selfish instincts, even though he had family responsibilities.'

I felt a great sense of peace flood through me. After all this time I'd managed to face up to my father and, not only that, had had the strength of faith to forgive him. But that didn't mean that I was going to persuade Joe to stay in The Community. That would be going too far.

'Have you anywhere to go when you leave here, Dad? Do you want me to ring anyone?'

'I suppose I could go to Kelly's but, don't bother yourself, son, I'll sort it out—you're probably too goody-goody to have anything to do with her either. Right sanctimonious little prig you turned out to be!'

'Okay, if that's what you want.'

I put my hand out to shake his. Dad started to say something and I hoped that he was going to show some sign of repentance.

'Wouldn't mind a lift into town though, if you can sort it out. It's a long walk you know.'


I waved him off as Paul drove him into town. I felt like a part of me had been washed away and I was cleaner inside as a result. Jess came out to the front door and took my hand to lead me inside for dinner. We managed to find a place to sit where we weren't surrounded by the others and I felt so happy, sitting with Jess and talking about the baby we were expecting.

Elijah took Circle Time that evening. He seemed subdued, but everyone else carried on as normal. At the end, he and Rebecca smiled at each other; she took his hand and they went to Social Hour together.

# Thirty Two

Jess's birthday. Not something we celebrated at The Larches, but no one could tell us what to do in our own room. I'd hidden some freesias in my drawer the night before. Maybe I should have thought it through a little more, my underwear smelt of flowers for weeks.

Anyway, I put the flowers on the bedside table as soon as I woke. Jess was still sleeping peacefully; I slipped downstairs and made her a tray with tea, a boiled egg, toast and some of Liz's home made jam. I ate the first two slices of toast while the egg was boiling; I was starving. Then I got all nervous waiting for the next two to pop up, worried that the egg would get cold.

It was about six am, early for Jess, but I wanted to have some quiet time together before the chaos of the day started. Back up in the room, I shook her shoulder gently until she opened her eyes.

'What?'

'Happy Birthday! It's a big one today, thirty years old.'

'Don't remind me.'

I laughed. 'You'll always be younger than me, however long we both live.'

'S'pose that's true. What time is it?'

'Six oh seven.'

'Oh, too early, too early.'

She snuggled back down. I shook her shoulder again.

'Look, I've made you breakfast.'

She woke properly this time. 'Oh, that's sweet.' She pulled herself up and I propped the pillows behind her. She gave me a taste of her boiled egg, but pulled the spoon away when I tried to have some more.

'It's mine; keep your mitts off it.'

When she'd finished, I put the tray on the floor and sat next to her on the bed, my arm around her waist. She rested her head on my shoulder.

'This is nice,' she said, 'let's do this every day.'

'Only if we take turns.'

'No, it should be your turn every day. I am pregnant after all.'

'Really, I hadn't noticed!'

I stroked her tummy. Wouldn't be long now. As the date got nearer and nearer, I worried more and more. How would we manage without medical attention? I daren't talk to Jess any more about it, we'd been over and over it and there seemed to be no solution.

'How's Rebecca doing?' I asked to get my mind away from worries about the birth.

'She's a lot brighter now but...' Jess stopped talking and gazed off into the distance, looking worried.

'But what?'

'She told me what the arguing was about. I promised myself I wouldn't tell you about it, but I have to tell someone and I know I can trust you.'

'Yes you can. What was it about?'

'Elijah thinks she's having an affair with George.'

'George? That doesn't sound very likely to me. Not likely at all. Why does he think that?'

'She was upset one day and George was comforting her. He had his arm round her shoulders and Rebecca was saying she was worried because she wasn't pregnant after all this time. Elijah came in the room and saw them. He must have heard a little of what George was saying because, as soon as they were alone, he accused her of trying to seduce George so that she could get pregnant.'

'That's ridiculous.'

'I know, but Elijah is so wound up about the whole thing he doesn't seem able to see sense.'

'Has Rebecca persuaded him that he's wrong?'

'Sometimes he says he trusts her, but the smallest thing has to happen and he's off again. Like the other day, when he ran off, he'd seen George following Rebecca down the corridor and he presumed they were going off to be alone together.'

'And they weren't?'

'Liam, you're as bad as Elijah! No they weren't. They were going to plan a lesson that George was giving to the children, on the history of The Larches.'

'I didn't really think they were having an affair.'

'I should hope not.'

I looked at the clock. It was time for me to go and have a little more breakfast then start getting ready for the deliveries, but I decided to have another half an hour with Jess.

That turned out to be a mistake. Methuselah had been locked in the greenhouse over night and it took me ages to clear up the mess. I was behind schedule all day, which made me almost as irritable as Elijah.

# Thirty Three

'Liam.'

I opened my eyes but it was still very dark so I closed them again, presuming I'd been dreaming.

'Liam, wake up.'

I propped myself up on one elbow. 'What?'

'The bed's wet. There's something wrong—maybe my waters have broken.'

'But you're not due yet.'

'I know that but it doesn't stop me being scared. Put the light on.'

I threw myself out of bed quickly. I turned the light on, but it was so bright it hurt my eyes so I closed them for a minute. When I opened them, Jess had pushed the covers back. The sheet under her was bright red. Scarily red.

'It's blood, Liam, look at it. Blood. What are we going to do?'

'I'll have to take you to hospital.'

'But we're not allowed. What's Elijah going to say?'

'Never mind what he says. We can't take risks with our baby.'

I dressed as quickly as I could and wrapped Jess in the quilt before picking her up. I struggled to open the door and carried Jess down the two flights as quietly as I could, panicking every time a stair squeaked. When we got to the front door I realised I should have brought the key down. I sat Jess on a chair in the hallway and went in the office for the spare but, as I reached up to take it from the hook, Elijah appeared behind me.

'Going somewhere?'

'I'm taking Jess to the hospital, she's bleeding.'

'You're not taking her anywhere. The Lord will take care of her.'

'I'm not risking it.'

'You'll stay here. Take Jess back upstairs.'

'No, I'm taking her.'

'If you don't carry her back upstairs this minute, then I will.' He set off in Jess's direction.

There was no way was I going to let him stop us getting help for Jess and the baby. I bunched up my fist and swung it at him. I'm not much of a fighter, but I was so scared I must have found some extra strength because it was such a powerful punch, he took several steps backwards against the desk and ended up lying on it with his legs in the air. I didn't stop to check if he was hurt, just ran from the office, opened the front door and picked up Jess, locking the door behind me, so Elijah would have to find another key before he could come after us.

I settled Jess in the passenger seat and then set off for the hospital. Something struck me as we drove along the darkened country lanes.

'Does it hurt?'

'No, there's no pain at all.'

'Maybe that means it's okay.'

'Maybe.'

We were both quiet then until I had to stop at traffic lights on the edge of Burnley.

'Liam, what if we lose the baby?'

'We won't lose the baby. God won't let us lose the baby.'

I really hoped that was true.

'What if Elijah's right and we're going against God's will by going to the hospital?'

'How can it be against his will when so many babies are born there?'

'I hope you're right.'

We were at the Burnley General Hospital by then. I headed for Urgent Care because I didn't know where else to take Jess. I parked at the door and carried her in. A nurse helped her into a wheelchair and asked me to move the van from the door. I ran out and found a parking space as quickly as possible but, by the time I'd got back, Jess had disappeared. I went to the reception desk.

'Do you know where Jess Donnelly has gone?'

'They've taken her up to the Women's Centre.'

She gave me instructions how to get there, but I must not have listened because I got lost. Very lost. Later I couldn't understand how I managed to end up wandering down endless corridors because it was quite an easy route.

The air in the hospital was hot and heavy, muffling my footsteps so I felt like I was walking on cotton wool. There was very little light in the corridors. Outside the windows everything was very black and my reflection was mirrored on either side of the corridor. My heart was beating hard and I wondered if I'd ever find anyone to help me find the way.

Eventually I found the hospital canteen and I went in. There were lights at one end of a very big room filled with tables and two nurses were drinking coffee and talking.

'Can you help me please? I'm lost.'

They both looked up surprised. One of them gasped loudly. I looked down at my shirt which was covered with blood, presuming it was that which had caused the gasp. But it wasn't.

'Liam!'

It was Kirsty. God must have sent her to look after me.

'What's happened?'

'It's Jess. She's having a baby and she was bleeding so I brought her in. They've taken her up to the Women's

173

Centre but I've got lost and I can't find her.' My voice cracked and I thought I was going to cry. 'I've lost her.'

'Come on, I'll take you.'

She held on to my arm on the way up to the ward and kept talking all the time to try to calm me down. It worked, a little bit anyway. She'd had a son who she'd called Liam. That really pleased me.

The sister on the ward told us that Jess had been taken for an emergency Caesarean because there were problems that had caused the bleeding. They were fairly certain the baby would be fine though. She said I could wait in the day room for news. Kirsty took me in there.

'I've got to go back to my ward now. Sister'll be going bananas. I'll come back up when I'm off duty. If you want me to, that is.'

I was very scared and felt like I needed as much support as I could get. 'I do want you to.'

Kirsty gave me a hug and went back down to her ward. A nurse brought me a cup of tea although, for the first time in a long time, I would have liked something stronger. I seemed to be sat there for a long time, nothing to do, no one to talk to until Sister came in to talk to me.

'It's a little girl, Mr Donnelly. Five pounds six ounces. Not a bad size considering she's so early. They're taking her to the Neonatal Intensive Care Unit. We'll take you down to see her as soon as we can.'

'And Jess?'

'She's lost a lot of blood so we'll have to do a transfusion. But apart from that she's fine. She'll be coming back up to the ward soon.'

'Thanks, Sister. Will you tell me when I can see her, see both of them?'

'Of course we will, Mr Donnelly.'

She turned to go, then turned back.

'Oh by the way, Kirsty rang and we told her about the baby, hope that was okay. She said she'd come up when her shift ends.'

'That's great.'

'If there's anyone else you want to tell, there's a public phone at the end of the corridor.'

I shook my head. I daren't ring The Larches in case Elijah answered. I'd have to face the music when I went back, but I wasn't ready for that yet. I was too excited about the baby and worried about Jess.

I sat down. Stood up. Sat down. My legs were twitchy so I couldn't sit still. I stood up again and went over to the window. The hospital was just starting the day. Vans making deliveries. Porters pushing trolleys. Nurses arriving for work, others going home. It was only a couple of storeys beneath my feet, but it felt like another world out there.

In the Day Room it was hot. I felt like I was wrapped in a thick scratchy blanket and my hair was heavy on my head. I opened a window and as I was gasping in the fresh air like a fish, someone touched me on the shoulder. It was Kirsty.

'Sister asked me to tell you Jess is ready for you to see her. Come on, I'll show you where she is.'

She took hold of my hand and led me to a room behind Sister's desk. I hesitated in the doorway, but when I saw Jess there with a drip up, I rushed towards her. Then I didn't know whether I could touch her or not so I stopped about a foot from the bed.

'It's alright, Liam, I won't break. I'm just a bit sore on my tummy that's all.'

Her voice was a little slurry, probably from the anaesthetic. I knelt down by the bed, being careful not to knock it; then I reached out and stroked her face.

'Are you really alright?'

175

'Will be when I can see the baby. Sister says I have to wait until I'm a bit stronger before they can take me down. She said you can go down in a few minutes.'

'I'll tell you exactly what she looks like, I promise. Can't wait till we can all be together.'

I heard a rustle at the doorway and realised Kirsty was still there.

'Jess, this is my sister Kirsty. She helped me last night.'

Kirsty came in, but then hesitated.

'Is it alright me being here, Jess? Liam said he's not supposed to have contact with his family.'

Jess grinned. 'We're already in a lot of trouble. I don't think this will make much difference.'

Jess lifted her arms awkwardly to welcome Kirsty in a hug.

'Liam's told the baby all about you and Kelly; I overheard what he said while he was whispering to the baby. He loved you a lot and being in The Community doesn't mean he's forgotten you two. Or Steven.'

It felt so good seeing my wife and sister together.

A nurse came in. 'I'll take you down to see the baby now, Mr Donnelly.'

'Wish you could come, Jess.'

'Me too but I'll just have to wait a little while.'

When we got to the Neonatal Unit, I had to put on a special gown and mask to protect the babies from germs. Then Sister took me down to the far end of the unit to see our baby. I couldn't believe that anyone so tiny could exist.

'You can hold her for a minute Mr Donnelly.'

She was like a bundle of cotton wool in my arms. Her eyes were closed and she looked just like Jess when she's sleeping. She kept putting out her pink tongue and licking her lips. I tickled the middle of her hand with my finger and she grasped it for a moment. This was my baby, our daughter; I felt so proud.

'What are you going to call her?'

'Last time we talked we thought about Amanda for a girl, but I'm so happy she's here I'm going to ask Jess if we can call her Hosanna Joy.'

'That's an unusual name but it will certainly make her feel welcome in the world.'

Sister held out her arms to put the baby back in her incubator. I kissed her on her smooth forehead and handed her over. I stood and watched whilst Sister settled her down.

'I'm afraid you'll have to go now Mr Donnelly. We want to carry out some tests on little Hosanna here.'

I changed out of my gown and went back to the ward, dying to ask Jess about the name. I couldn't ask though because she was asleep. Kirsty was still there.

'Just wanted to check how everything is. How's the baby?'

'She's beautiful.'

I gave Kirsty a lift home and went in for coffee. I got a chance to meet Matt and their little boy. They made a lovely family.

Then back home to face the music. Tom was on duty at the gatehouse. 'Elijah won't tell us what went on last night, but it looks like you and Jess are in a lot of trouble. Where is Jess by the way?'

'She's in the hospital. We've had a little girl.'

'No wonder you're in trouble. Congratulations anyway and good luck—you're going to need it.'

Elijah was waiting for me. He was very angry and, at first, he threatened to throw us both out, but he gradually calmed down and said I hadn't to have any contact with the others for the next week as punishment for disobeying him. I was to eat alone, work alone and pray alone. That was fine with me.

Then he said, 'And I don't want you to go visiting that hospital. Jess obviously has to stay there till she's better and she can bring the baby home, but I don't want you to go up there.'

'I can't agree with that, Elijah. I can't leave them there all alone; I have to keep visiting them. If you stop me I'll leave and take the two of them with me.'

There was a silence in the room although my head was full of buzzing panic. What would we do? Where would we go? How would we manage?

'Very well then, but you'll have to take up extra duties to make up for that time. Do you understand me?'

'Yes, Elijah'

'I'll get George to allocate you some work that you can do alone.'

So no one spoke to me whilst Jess was in hospital, although everyone gave me sympathetic looks in passing. I ate in my room and did my rounds on my own. George pushed notes under the bedroom door each evening telling me which extra jobs I should do—mainly peeling potatoes and scrubbing floors. But I didn't mind because I could go and see Jess and the baby, our baby, whenever I wanted.

Jess agreed that Hosanna Joy was the right name for our new baby. It was a bit of a mouthful though so we decided to call her Hanna for short.

# Thirty Four

Hanna was in the Neonatal Unit for eight days, then she spent a couple of days with Jess on the ward. When the doctor said that they could come home I was so excited.

As I walked on the ward my heart was beating so loudly and I felt like I couldn't breathe. This was it, my own little family. But I didn't say that to anyone, even Jess, because I wasn't supposed to feel like that, we were all one big family at The Larches. I'd taken a bunch of my best flowers for the staff and Jess carried them down to hand over to the Sister.

I looked down at little Hosanna Joy. She was dressed in her going home clothes; a pink all-in-one outfit which Jess told me was a Babygro. It had a blue embroidered teddy bear on it. Jess said it was a present from Kirsty and warned me not to mention that. Hanna looked so beautiful, but I was still frightened of picking her up in case I hurt or scared her.

Then Jess came back and picked Hanna up. Hanna half opened one eye and smiled. 'Look she's smiling,' I said excitedly to Jess.

A passing nurse muttered, 'Wind,' but we knew differently. Hanna was happy to be going home.

Back at the house the gate was covered with balloons and there was a huge sign over the front door saying, 'Welcome Home, Hosanna Joy Donnelly!' Elijah must have forgiven us because he was the only one I'd told the name.

When they heard the car everyone came out on the steps and gave a big cheer. Hanna blinked at the loud noise and the bright sunlight, but she didn't cry. She knew there was nothing to be frightened of at The Larches.

Inside the baby was handed from one to another so that they could all admire her. Rachel said she was jealous that Jess had got it over with and she still had a while to go. No one mentioned the hospital or the fact that they hadn't been allowed to speak to me whilst Jess was in there.

After everyone had held Hanna, Elijah suggested that we go up to our room for a rest and to settle Hanna in. We went upstairs, promising the children that we'd bring Hanna back down soon to see them.

Everything was ready in our room for Hanna to move in. There was a Moses basket which Andrea had found in a second hand shop when she went out on her mission work. She'd also got us some bottles and a second hand steriliser for the bottles. Rachel had sewn covers and a pretty yellow quilt for the basket and there was a selection of clothes—I never found out where they came from. I had been worried about all these things because I had no money and I hadn't been able to talk about my worries to anyone, but Jess had reassured me that someone would sort it out.

Jess put Hanna down in the basket and she went straight to sleep. Then Jess took my hand and pulled me to sit down on the bed with her. She leant her head against my shoulder and I rested my head gently against hers. I felt so happy until I realised my shoulder was wet. Jess was crying. I put my finger under her chin and tilted her face up to mine.

'What's wrong, love?'

'Nothing. Everything. I've got to dress my brand new baby in second hand clothes. She's going to sleep in a second hand laundry basket. All the sheets are old ones that someone's cut up to make them the same size. We haven't even got a pram. Not only that, they all think they know best. They'll be telling us what to do. Maybe *he'll* make her sleep in the nursery with the other girls before we're ready for that.'

'We'll sort it, don't worry. Everything's going to be strange for a while, but it will settle down. Come on now, you're tired after all this excitement. Have a little sleep while Hanna's asleep, you'll need your energy when she wakes up.'

We lay down side by side on the bed and I held Jess in my arms till she went to sleep. She wasn't the only one who was worried.


But it wasn't just on that first day that Jess cried. She cried all the time. I didn't know how to cope with this new Jess. She'd always been the strong one and now she looked to me to make all the decisions. Should she carry on breast feeding? Was it wrong to get up in the night whenever Hanna cried? Whatever we did, she became convinced it was the wrong thing.

Hanna seemed to be picking up on her distress so she cried a lot as well. Some nights no one slept in our room. Then, in the morning, Jess didn't want to get out of bed. She'd ask me to give her Hanna, she'd feed her and then they both went back to sleep in bed until the next feed at ten. Liz would be furious when Jess went down to the kitchen asking for breakfast at eleven.

I got more and more tired. Everyone kept offering me advice.

'Be strict with Jess. In the morning, she should get up and dressed before feeding Hanna, then four hourly feeds until ten at night. No sleeping for Jess during the day and, at night, if the baby cries Jess should give her a drink of water and put her straight back in the cot. No mollycoddling and Hanna will soon get in a routine.' That was George.

'Ignore George,' said Ruth who'd found an old baby book behind a cupboard in the attic. 'You must feed Hanna on demand. Let Jess get as much rest as she needs. The two have to bond, nothing else matters.'

'No, that's not right.' Rebecca told me. 'Change Hanna's feeding times so she wakes at 8 in the morning. Then the last feed will be at midnight and, fingers crossed, she should sleep right through and Jess can get up at a normal time. That's what happened with Becky.'

I had no idea who was right, although I felt that, if Jess could get herself stronger, she'd know exactly what to do. One day, as I arrived back from my rounds, Elijah asked to have a word with me.

'How's it going with the baby, Liam?'

It seemed to be the right time for honesty. 'Doesn't seem to be going very well. Jess keeps crying and she's not coping at all.'

'A few people have told me that they think Jess has the baby blues. What do you think?'

I thought about it. I didn't know much about the baby blues, but Jess had had problems since Hanna was born so it might be that.

'Could be. She's certainly very down. Not sure what we could do about it though.'

'Rebecca's had a look at that baby book of Ruth's. It says that depression like this is very common with new mothers. Sometimes it can go on to becoming full-blown depression. We don't want that to happen.'

'But what can I do?'

'Well, I think one of the first things to do is to stop everyone bothering Jess. Just let her get on with learning to be a mother. Tell you what; don't go to Afternoon Assembly today. Just spend some time in your room together and I'll have a word with everyone asking them to leave you both alone for a while.'

'That sounds good. Thanks for that. At least we won't have to worry about what everyone thinks.'

'Right. Now let's think what else might help. Is there anything she's particularly worried about?'

I hesitated. 'She's upset that everything the baby has is second hand. All she has that's new is that babygro that …' I stopped himself in time from saying 'Kirsty', 'someone on the ward gave her.'

'I think the budget will stretch to some new things for the baby. In fact, that might be a good idea for all the babies. Tell you what, how about the two of you taking a trip into town with fifty pounds to spend on the baby? Anything that Jess wants to get. Do you think she'd like that?'

'I think she'd love that.'

'How does she feel about going back to work? I know she's not ready yet, but do you think that's worrying her?'

'It's one of the things she's mentioned.' She'd actually said she couldn't face going back to teaching that group of horrors, but I didn't want to tell Elijah that.

'I suppose it would be a bit over facing. Don't tell her we've been talking, but let her know she doesn't have to go back to teaching until she's absolutely ready. We're coping now with the teaching rota and we can carry on as long as necessary. When it's time, maybe she can go back slowly, just mornings to start, or one-to-one teaching. I know Becky could do with some extra help with her spelling.'

'Okay. Thanks a lot Elijah.'

It surprised me that he was so understanding, but I was grateful for it.

# Thirty Five

It was strange to be out in town with Jess. She was excited but nervous.

'The cars go so fast. They whoosh in my ears.'

'Come on my other side then, so I'm between you and the road.'

I stood still while she changed sides. She clung on to my hand; it wasn't only the cars that were a problem.

'Too many people, Liam, and they all walk so fast.'

'Don't take any notice of them. Just concentrate on walking with me.'

Her fingers tightened against mine. I'd got used to being out and about, but she'd spent so much time inside The Larches' walls that the hustle and bustle of the town centre was too much for her. I was worried that her trip out would make her worse, not better.

'Come on, we'll have a look in this shop. It looks quite quiet.'

The shop was full of baby things: clothes, cots, prams, nappies, bottles, toys. Jess wandered into the section where the cots were. She stroked the shiny wood surface longingly.

'This is so beautiful. Can you imagine Hanna snuggling down in this?' She looked at the price tag. 'Oh no, it's two hundred pounds. Just for a cot. And we've only got fifty pounds.' Her face took on a determined look. 'Let's find something else.'

The something else was a dress. It took a long time. She'd pick up a dress, stroke it, touch the fabric against her face, hold it at arm's length, put it in the basket and then take it out again because she'd seen another one even prettier. At one point she had two in the basket but, ever practical, she decided that it was more sensible to buy other more everyday items. Next we found a bargain basket full of baby vests. She picked up four, two to fit Hanna as she was, two more to grow into. Then her eye was caught by the baby carriers.

'Look at these, look, Liam, look!'

'I'm looking. What are they?'

'They're slings, silly! You put them on your shoulders and then carry the baby in them. It means that Hanna can be with me whatever I'm doing and I'll still have my hands free.' She read the instructions. 'Oh, and I can choose whether she faces towards me or if she wants to, she can face outwards and watch what's going on.'

'How much are they?'

'This one's forty pounds. That's too much. Wonder if there are any cheaper ones?'

We searched the shelves. I found one at eighteen pounds. Jess examined it closely.

'Do you think it's still safe? Even though it's cheap. I wouldn't want to take risks with Hanna.'

A passing shop assistant reassured us that all their carriers passed the necessary safety standards. The carrier went into the basket with the vests and the dress. We still had a little money left. Jess picked up a colourful baby toy that had four spinners on it. Then it was back to the bargain basket where she found some pink frilly rubber pants to go over Hanna's nappies. The bill came to forty nine pounds fifty and we were very proud of ourselves for getting so near our target amount. Then Jess spotted some colourful transfers of nursery characters to stick above Hanna's cot. Reduced. Fifty pence. She picked them up and rushed back to the till.

On the way home, Jess was quiet.

'Are you okay?'

'I'm feeling good. We got some nice things for Hanna didn't we?'

'We certainly did.'

# Thirty Six

Jess had been feeling better; the trip out seemed to make a big difference and she loved to dress Hanna up in her new dress and frilly pants on Sundays for Special Assembly. She used the carrier every day, most of the time keeping Hanna facing outwards so that she could see everyone and everything. Hanna seemed to like it best when Jess was working in the greenhouse—Jess thought it was because of the brightly coloured flowers. Then when she was listening to someone reading or marking books, she turned Hanna round so she could rest her head on Jess's breast and go to sleep.

But then Jess had a bad day. Hanna had been awake all night and Jess was worried about her. Later, during Becky's reading lesson, Jess had been a little sharp with her and Becky lost her temper, shouting, 'I hate you, I hate you, you're no good as a teacher now you've had the baby.' Jess was so upset at that her hand went out to smack her. She stopped herself just in time and sent Becky to sit in the hallway facing the wall.

In the afternoon, when Jess went to work in the greenhouse, Methuselah had sneaked in behind her and knocked over a lot of plants which then had to be repotted. At dinner time, Jess caught her hand against her plate, knocking it to the floor. It smashed into pieces and gravy and mashed potatoes splattered all over Jess's legs and the walls. She put her head on the table and began crying. I went to comfort her as her sobs became louder and louder, but Elijah reached her first and stood behind her with his hands on her shoulders. Everyone was watching and the room quietened. Even Jess's sobs quietened and developed a regular heartbeat-like rhythm.

Elijah spoke in a strong loud voice. 'This poor woman has been invaded by the devil. He must have afflicted her soul when she went into the hospital against God's will.' Elijah stopped and glared at me. 'We will exorcise this devil from her soul. Tonight will be a special Assembly where, together, we will pray to save our poor Jess.'

Elijah walked into the Assembly Room and stood at the front.

'Tonight we're going to exorcise the devil from Jess's soul. He's draining her strength and she's struggling to live her usual God-fearing life. She has a child to care for and her part to play within our Community. She needs to be rid of this evil so that she can enjoy her life again and be amongst us properly.'

He signalled to Jess to come to him and kneel. He put his hands on her shoulders and stared upwards.

'Lord God, help us save our beloved Jess. Help us expunge the devil from her soul. Cleanse her and return to us the happy Jess that we knew.'

He turned his head towards the rest of The Community. 'Help me. Help me save Jess. I want you all to join in my appeal to God on Jess's behalf. Repeat after me, 'May the devil be gone!'

Everyone repeated, like one voice, 'May the Devil be gone!'

Elijah began a chant of 'May the Devil be gone!' and everyone repeated his words. Their voices became louder and louder; the air in the room pulsed with the heavy words. Jess began to toss her head wildly from side to side, her body heaving as the words washed over her. Tears flowed down her face and her cheeks shone in the light that suddenly seemed harsh and blinding above us.

I wasn't convinced that this was the way to treat Jess, but I was willing to give it a try. I joined in with the chant. It drew me in and soon my words were as loud, if not louder, than the rest. It felt like those words were the only things in the entire world, like they'd go on forever.

Suddenly, Jess screamed and collapsed face first on to the floor. The chant slowed and then stopped. Elijah knelt down and gently stroked Jess's face then stood to face everyone.

'Hallelujah! The devil has gone and Jess has returned to us.'

Free from the chant, I could see that wasn't *my* Jess on the floor. My Jess should be standing up tall; she didn't lie on the floor. I went to the front and picked her up. Her face was pale and her body limp; one arm swung against my side as I carried her from the room to the sound of The Community's singing of, 'Praise my Soul the King of Heaven.'

Upstairs I gently laid her on the bed. There was more colour in her face, but she was still very pale. Her eyes flickered open.

'What happened? What am I doing in bed?'

She tried to get up but I put out a hand to stop her.

'Stay there and get some rest. We went to the exorcism, remember?'

'Oh yes. I remember now.'

'How are you feeling?'

'Very strange. Sort of empty. Bit like a deflated balloon.'

'I think you need some rest. Let's get you undressed and into bed.'

When she was under the covers, I kissed her gently on the forehead.

'Do you want me to stay with you?'

'No, I'll probably be better on my own for a little while. I'm ready to go to sleep.'

'Okay, I'll come back up in an hour to check on you. Sleep tight.'

I stroked her hair and then left the room. When I got downstairs I could hear they were still singing in the Assembly Room, but I didn't feel I could face them just then. I went to the Social Room where Rebecca was looking after Hanna and I spent the next hour holding Hanna in my arms and talking to her about all sorts of things.

I don't think that exorcism was needed at all. Jess had been through a lot and women often get down after they've had a baby. She was doing fine, just had a bad day that's all. If you're feeling bad, the last thing you need is lots of people chanting at you. It could have made her worse, not better.

It was strange the way Elijah suddenly decided it was the devil causing the problem. He'd never mentioned that before and had been fine about her depression, looking for ways to make things easier for her and talking to me about it. Than all of a sudden, he started going on about devils and exorcism.

There were a few times when he did strange things round then. He made Liz cut down on her food budget, saying we were all eating too much. We had to stop having puddings and there was only bread and margarine if we were still hungry after the main course. After three or four weeks, he decided we all needed building up and told George to give Liz extra money to stock up. And one day he even gave Liz the day off and sent out for pizza for us all. Everybody really enjoyed that, but it put ideas in the children's heads and they kept asking for us to do it again.

And poor Becky. One minute he made her go to bed at six o'clock because she wasn't getting enough sleep and then he'd encourage her to stay up after social hour to play Monopoly with him. Some days she wasn't allowed to play outside in case she hurt herself and other days he'd tell her to get outside and climb trees so she could toughen up.

I wondered if the responsibility of running The Larches, along with his concerns about his relationship with Rebecca, was getting to him. There were a lot of us and we were always going to him with our worries. Still, it wasn't as though he didn't have God to turn to and, if he wanted help from us, he only had to ask.

# Thirty Seven

I don't know if it was a coincidence or not but a midwife joined The Community before the other three babies were born. Her name was Mary and she was great: calm, organised and very sensible. I wish she'd been around when Hanna was born, although, as she said to me, we'd still have had to go to the hospital for the Caesarean.

The first to give birth was Andrea. She started in labour in the Social Room one Friday evening. Mary had arranged one of the small bedrooms upstairs as a birthing room: it was a difficult job getting Andrea up there as she insisted on walking but kept having to sit down on the stairs. Once she was in there, everything moved very quickly, according to Jess who had offered to help Mary. It was so quick that we only just managed to get Will in from the gatehouse in time. They called the baby Joseph William. He had bright red hair and was a very noisy baby from the start.

The next baby was Tom and Gemma's. They named her Adah Bethany. She was born early as Gemma had a fall, which started her in labour. Adah was very tiny and for a while we feared we'd lose her, but with the constant love and care of us all, she soon began to thrive.

Finally, Emmanuel Paul was born to Ruth and Paul. He was a very quiet baby who watched the world with big eyes and seemed to understand everything that was said to him.

The house looked to be full of babies, prams, cots, nappies and all the other things that it takes to look after such tiny creatures. In the end we decided to set up a kind of nursery on the ground floor so that the babies could spend most of the day in there, surrounded by all their equipment. It also made more sense for the new mothers to share the child care during the day, although the babies still slept in with their parents at night.

Jess found a new role when the other babies were born. She was the experienced mother and so the others often came to her with their questions. It helped her over her depression as she realised how the others had noticed that she was good with Hanna. This was a very happy time for Jess and I was so glad to see her back to her old self again.

And Hanna became more beautiful every day. She was so quick, walking and talking early, and she had a smile for everyone. We were so proud of her.

Paul went out and bought a digital camera so we could start taking photographs, not just of the babies, but of everyone. Now I had a photo album I could go to, one that showed the passing of time and how happy our lives could be in that house.

# Thirty Eight

It was a cold and rainy day and I'd done all the work possible in the greenhouse for that day so I headed back to the house. On my way I saw Becky sitting in the middle of the lawn: she had no coat on and she looked absolutely drenched through.

'What on earth are you doing, Becky? Get inside this minute.'

'Elijah sent me out here so that the rain could wash away the badness in my soul. I've got to stay here till quarter to four.'

I looked at my watch. It was three thirty. 'Come on, let's get you inside, you don't need another quarter of an hour of this, you'll freeze to death.' I took off my coat and wrapped it around her. Inside the house I told her to go and have a bath and put on some dry clothes, promising to tell Liz to have some hot chocolate ready when she came down again. I called in the kitchen.

'Liz, Becky's been outside in the rain. I've sent her up for a bath. Do you think you could give her some hot chocolate when she comes down?'

'Course I will. What was she doing out in this weather?'

'Elijah sent her out there, some sort of punishment apparently. I'm going to have a word with him about it.'

I left the kitchen and set off for the office, but met Elijah in the corridor.

'Have you seen Becky?'

'I sent her up for a bath. She was soaked through. I was just coming to talk to you about it.'

'How dare you countermand my orders? I sent her out there to rid her of the devil in her soul, which makes her so disobedient and cheeky towards me. I'd told her not to jump down the stairs, that it's too dangerous. So she ignores me and then comes crying because she's hurt her knee. She's nearly seven years old, old enough to know better, it has to be the devil that makes her like she is.'

'She's still only a child, Elijah. It was very cold out there and I'm sure she's learnt her lesson.'

Elijah made his hand into a fist and banged it against the wall.

'We can't allow the devil to rule here. It's bad enough out there in the world. We have to protect ourselves because, if we don't, if we don't...' Elijah's face worked with emotion and he used a finger to wipe his cheek. 'If we don't, we could lose everything we have here.' Again he banged the wall. 'Everything! I... will... not... let... that... happen.'

He set off down the corridor; then he turned round and waved his fist in the air. 'And if it does happen, it will be your fault, Liam, for allowing the devil to remain within Becky's soul.'


My sending Becky in early didn't stop her becoming ill. The day after, Jess noticed that she was looking pale and, when she asked how she was feeling, Becky said she had a sore throat. Mary looked at her and said she would be better off in bed. Rebecca took her upstairs and Mary brought her a honey and lemon drink from the kitchen.

When I called in later that afternoon to see how she was, she was awake but her eyes were glazed over and she was muttering about how she needed to get out of bed to look for Methuselah's tail because a mouse had stolen it. When I put my hand on her forehead, I could tell she had a high temperature so I went to the top of the stairs and shouted for someone to find Mary.

Mary was very worried when she saw Becky's condition. She wanted to send for a doctor straightaway.

Rebecca, even though she was worried about Becky, was more worried about how Elijah would react if they did that. Mary agreed that we would try to break the fever ourselves, but insisted that, if Becky got any worse, the doctor would have to be called. She didn't want to be responsible for what would happen if they delayed.

We found some old towels and a basin of cold water and Rebecca sat by Becky's side, sponging her down. By evening, Becky seemed to be sleeping more calmly and her temperature had dropped. Rebecca still wanted to stay by her bedside and it was agreed that the other girls from Becky's room would be found alternative beds for the night so they wouldn't be disturbed by Rebecca being there.

When I was on my way up to bed, I opened Becky's bedroom door quietly to check everything was alright. Inside, Elijah was pulling on Rebecca's arm, trying to move her away from the bed. He let go as the door opened and they both turned to look at me. Rebecca put on a forced smile and said, 'She seems to be a lot better now, Liam. No need to worry any more, you get along to bed.'

I smiled and closed the door and, almost immediately, I heard their raised voices.

'Come on, Rebecca, your place is in bed with me.'

'I'm staying here tonight, she's my daughter, I can't leave her alone when she's been so ill.'

'But she's alright now, she doesn't need you. I do. Come on, Rebecca, you know what will happen if you don't.'

'There's nothing more you can do to scare me.'

'You'll regret this. I'm off to bed now, if you aren't up there by midnight, you'll be sorry.'

'Good night, Elijah, see you in the morning.'

As I heard him heading to the door I raced off upstairs so he wouldn't know I'd been listening.

# Thirty Nine

I was up early the next morning; there was no particular reason apart from the promise of good weather after a week of cold rain. As I set off down the attic stairs I thought I heard a shuffling noise before the linen cupboard door opened and closed. The younger children had been known to use good sheets to make tents in the garden and I wanted to make sure they weren't on an early morning raid. I went to investigate.

Inside I found Rebecca. Her face was covered in cuts and bruises and her left arm was hanging at a funny angle.

'What happened to you?'

'I fell down the stairs,' she mumbled. Her lip was split and it looked like she'd broken some teeth.

'So why are you hiding in here?'

'Er, bandages, I need bandages for my arm.'

'You need hospital, that's what you need. Come on, I'll take you in the van.'

'No, I can't, you know I can't. What will Elijah say?'

'Did he do this? Elijah?'

'No, I told you, I fell down the stairs.'

'Well, however it happened, that arm's not going to get better on its own. And those cuts on your face need looking at too. I'm taking you to Casualty and no argument.'

I put my arm round her waist, helped her down the stairs and out to the van. As we drove I tried again to get her to tell me what had happened, but she still insisted that she had fallen downstairs.

When we got to the Urgent Care Centre that was what she told the receptionist. Even though she wrote it down, I could tell by the look on her face that she didn't believe it either. The doctor who examined Rebecca was concerned about a cut on the back of her head and insisted that she be transferred to Royal Blackburn Hospital.

I followed the ambulance in the van and parked it in the car park. Inside, I was told she had been taken to set her arm and then she would be admitted. I decided to wait until she was on the ward before going back home. Whilst I was waiting I rang The Larches and told them where we were. Better to break the news first before going back, that was my reasoning.

I settled down with a cup of coffee from the machine and waited. Everything seems to take forever in these places, even I knew that. Eventually I heard someone call my name.

'Mr Donnelly? We're just going to take Rebecca to the ward and settle her in, if you'd like to come along with us.'

Rebecca was on a trolley. Her arm was in plaster and her cuts had been cleaned up. There were a couple of stitches above her eyebrow and some on her lip. She looked pale but she managed a small smile.

And then Elijah arrived. He flung open the door and screamed at the receptionist, 'Where's my wife? Where is she? I'm here to take her home; she's not staying in this place.'

Rebecca tried to climb off her trolley but the nurse wouldn't let her. I turned from side to side, trying to decide whether to confront Elijah or go to Rebecca. A security guard put his hand on Elijah's shoulder and asked, 'What's the problem?' Elijah pushed his hand away and, spotting Rebecca, turned in her direction.

'Off there. Come on! Get down.'

The security guard took hold of Elijah by both shoulders and, in a firm voice, said, 'I don't think that's a good idea, sir. What about going home and coming back for your wife tomorrow, when you've calmed down?'

Elijah took no notice. He tried to struggle from the guard's grasp then, having failed to do that, he stood perfectly still, appearing to have given in. Everyone had relaxed when Elijah suddenly swung his elbow down into the guard's stomach. Winded, the man took a step back and Elijah got away, sprinting towards Rebecca. Several nurses and porters formed a line in front of the trolley to protect Rebecca and I moved towards Elijah. When he saw me he became even angrier; he picked up a small table and threw it towards me. I dodged out of the way but it caught a glancing blow to someone in a wheelchair behind me.

Out of the corner of my eye I could see more security staff heading towards us. Elijah must have realised they were coming as he picked up one of a pair of crutches leaning against the wall. He swung it in front of him in a semi-circle, trying to prevent them approaching him. It hit one of them in the leg and there was a sharp cracking sound. This made the security men even more determined to stop him; they snatched the crutch away and overpowered him before locking him in a side room.


When I got back to the Larches, the whole place was in upheaval. No one seemed to be going about their daily tasks. Instead there were groups of people on the steps, in the doorway, in the hall and in the office, all of them with worried faces and some were crying. Jess was on the steps and, as soon as the car drew in, she came running over to me. 'Are you alright?' she kept asking, 'you didn't get hurt, did you?'

Paul came out from the house. He was the one who had taken my phone call and he told me that Elijah had become hysterical when he was given the news about Rebecca. He'd grabbed some car keys from their hook in the office, rushed from the building and driven off. The car he had taken was a battered old banger that we tried not to use; it wasn't very reliable and the brakes were defective. Paul had tried to stop Elijah, saying he was in no state to drive, but Elijah pushed him aside, leapt into the car and raced off down the drive at a speed that no one could believe.

I explained about Rebecca's condition and that they were keeping her in, at least for overnight and possibly longer, depending on some tests they planned to do. Paul looked worried and suggested we go somewhere private to talk.

We went into the small interview room off the main office. Jess insisted on coming in with us, Paul wasn't keen on her being there, but she was clinging to my arm like she'd never let me go and she promised not to interfere, nor pass on what we discussed.

Paul began talking before we even had chance to sit down.

'So what really happened, Liam? Did she fall downstairs?'

'To be honest I don't think she did. Her face is badly bruised, she has a split lip and some broken teeth; she looks like she's been beaten up. One of her arms has a bruise all round it as though someone has been holding on to it too tightly. The other one, the broken one, could have come from her falling downstairs, I suppose. It must have been Elijah, he was very angry last night when she didn't want to leave Becky's bedside.'

Jess broke in, 'They were arguing in the early hours. Think it was about two. I didn't really worry about it because it's happened a few times lately.'

'I've thought for a while that there was something going wrong between them,' Paul said, 'Rebecca seems to have been avoiding him as much as she could and, when I've heard him speak to her, he's had a sharpness in his voice that I've never heard before. There's other things too, he's not eating properly and he can't seem to settle to anything. I've been worried about him.'

'He's not sleeping either,' I added, 'whatever time I get up he's in the office, working he says, but he's usually staring off into the distance or pacing round and round.'

'He's...' Paul started to speak and then paused, 'He's been like this before, but it's a long time ago and we kept it hushed up. It was me he hit that time.'

I was surprised at first, but when I thought about it a bit more, I realised that I'd always felt that Elijah was capable of totally exploding. I wished Paul weren't there; then I could talk to Jess about it.

'He thinks Rebecca is sleeping with George,' Jess said, 'I wonder if that's why he's been so angry lately.'

'No,' Paul said, 'he surely can't be thinking that.'

Jess nodded, 'Yes, he does, Rebecca told me he thinks she's doing it to get pregnant. I guess he's feeling useless compared to everyone else.'

There was a knock on the door. It was Ruth.

'There's been a call to the gatehouse from the hospital. Elijah's been admitted to the secure psychiatric ward where he's been heavily sedated. They thought he was a danger to himself and to others. I've got a phone number to ring to talk to the ward.'

'Right, thanks, Ruth. Okay, Liam,' he turned his head, 'and Jess. I'd better get on with this.'

When I got to the door Paul called me back. 'Liam, I think you'd better go to the hospital and see if you can find the car that Elijah took. We don't want that thing cluttering up their car park and I'm not even sure if it's taxed and insured. If you get stopped, we'll have to deal with it, but best to try and avoid any trouble. Take Ian with you so he can drive the van back. Oh, and try not to tell the others too much.'

Jess and I had a quick hug in the office before we went outside to face the others. There were lots of questions, 'How's Rebecca?', 'Which stairs did she fall down?', 'Is Elijah at the hospital with her?' and 'When will they both be home?' We told them that everything was going to be fine, that Rebecca had to have her arm set and they should both be back soon. I didn't think that was true, but I had to tell them something.

Jess walked me to the door. I squeezed her hand and said I'd be back soon. Just as I was about to go outside, Mary shouted my name. She was coming down the stairs and I waited at the bottom for her.

'Liam, do you think you could have a word with Becky?'

'I'm a bit busy, Mary, I've got to go back to the hospital.'

'I understand that, but to be honest she's hysterical and I can't calm her down. I'm worried she'll make herself ill again. She's been asking for you. She thinks Rebecca has died and we're keeping it from her. She says she'll believe you because you always tell her the truth.'

'What on earth makes her think Rebecca is dead.'

'Think about it. For as long as she can remember, Rebecca has been there for her. She's never even left the grounds and then, suddenly, there's no Rebecca. I think Daniel may have something to do with it too, I left them alone for a minute or two.'

'Okay, I'll come and see if I can talk some sense into her.'

I followed Mary up the stairs and, even before we got to the top, I could hear Becky's sobs. As soon as I walked into the room she held up her arms towards me. I put out my arms to her too and held her for a minute. The sobs eased a little bit; then she pushed me away and looked up into my eyes.

'She's dead, isn't she? Mummy's dead.'

'No, sweetheart, she's not.'

'Are you sure? Are you really sure?'

'I am sure. I've just been with her. She fell down the stairs and broke her arm. The hospital has put a plaster cast on it. She's also got some cuts and bruises on her face, but otherwise she's fine.'

'Honest?'

'Honest.'

She was definitely calmer now. She settled back on her pillows and I gave her a tissue to wipe her face.

'Now, I've got things to do so I have to go back to the hospital. Are you going to be a good girl for Mary now?'

She sniffed and nodded at the same time.

'Promise?'

'Promise.'

At the bottom of the stairs I ran into Paul.

'I'll go up to the hospital with you. I'll see how Elijah is and what the hospital and the police have to say about it all. We might as well go in my car.'

We didn't talk much on our journey. I don't know about Paul, but my stomach was churning and I felt like my world had come to an end.

Paul parked the car and I paid for the ticket; he'd forgotten to bring any money. Then he headed for the psychiatric ward and I went to look for the old banger that Elijah had taken.

It wasn't hard to find. It was in a corner, left at a weird angle taking up two spaces and with a parking ticket stuck to the windscreen. I took the ticket and put it in my pocket to give to George. I inspected the car to see if there was any damage; I wasn't sure, but I thought there might have been a new dent on the wing. It was such a wreck I couldn't really tell.

I'd taken the spare keys from the office but I didn't need them because the usual keys were still in the ignition. I drove home as carefully as I could on the back roads. Luckily, I wasn't stopped.

I parked the car in the barn, thinking it was better if no one else was tempted to use it as it seemed unsafe for it to be on the road. Then I went into the kitchen in search of some sandwiches. The churning stomach had suddenly turned into a raging hunger.

That whole day had a strange, unreal feeling. We ate in dribs and drabs—Liz put out sandwiches, yogurt and fruit and we helped ourselves. No work got done. School had been cancelled and, while the children took the opportunity to play various games out on the lawn, the others drifted about looking lost.

# Forty

The next day was no better and what made it worse was the number of strangers who came to visit us.

First there were the Social Workers. Three of them. They arrived at the gatehouse and asked to see the children. Tom was on duty and he called Paul out from the gatehouse office where he was working. Paul took them back into the office so he could find out what it was all about. They told him there were concerns about the safety of the children because of the state of Rebecca and how Elijah had reacted at the hospital. Added to that, a nurse had overheard Rebecca talking in her sleep, something about Elijah hitting Becky.

Paul took them up to the house straight away. First he took them into the library where Jess was trying to teach a group of very restless children. Jess told me the children perked up when the strangers came in; they were ready for a distraction from the life cycle of a fly. The Social Workers talked to each child on their own—Paul found space in the house for them to do that.

When they'd finished talking to the children, one of them talked to Jess and the other two went up to see Becky. We don't know what any of the children, including Becky, said to the Social Workers, but they were obviously happy that there wasn't any danger.

They told Paul that everything seemed to be in order, but they would be making several unannounced visits in the future. Although he wasn't comfortable about that, he agreed because he had to.

As they were leaving, one of the Social Workers took a card out of her bag and pinned it to the noticeboard in the hallway. It gave contact information in case anyone had any concerns.

'And I expect that to stay there,' I heard her say as I came back in from doing my rounds.

As soon as they had gone, Paul called everybody into the Assembly Room and told them what had happened with Rebecca and Elijah. He said that Rebecca had fallen down the stairs and Elijah had become so upset at Rebecca being taken to the hospital that he'd had to be admitted to calm him down. He also told them about the Social Workers' visit, saying it was a routine visit and explained about the card on the notice board. He added that he didn't expect anyone to need to use it.

At the end of the meeting, he officially gave everyone the day off, but said he hoped they'd find useful tasks to carry out, like polishing the library floor and mowing the lawn.

I nipped down to the gatehouse to have a word with Tom to see if a parcel had arrived that I was waiting for. I was the one who let the next visitor in through the gate. It was the local GP. I took him up to talk to Paul in the main office. Paul nodded at him to sit down and asked me to stay too.

'How can we help, Dr Anderton?' Paul asked.

'Well, I hope you don't think I'm interfering. I've had a couple of calls about Elijah Ellis and Rebecca Wardle being at the hospital. Elijah is on my books and has been for some time.'

So Elijah could have health care but we couldn't. Typical!

'But Rebecca isn't and, when we checked, she doesn't seem to be signed up with any other doctor in the area. So I got the receptionist to look through our records and Elijah is the only one signed up with us. I know you are entitled to choose which GP you want to go to, but with a community of... how many have you got here?'

'About sixty,' Paul said, 'give or take a few.'

'Right. Sixty adults and children. You'd think at least some of that number would be signed up with the nearest GP. Not only that, I noticed nappies on the washing line. Have you got babies here?'

Paul hesitated and then nodded.

'Okay. Were they born here?'

'They were.'

'With a midwife present?'

'We have our own midwife.'

'Is she registered? Does the health visitor see the children? Have they had their inoculations?'

Paul took a deep breath and then shook his head.

'Were the births registered?'

'No.'

'Mr Goddard, this is all very serious. Why on earth aren't you looking after the people in your care?'

'Well, Elijah doesn't believe ...'

'Elijah hasn't shown himself to be the most responsible person in the world, has he? Screaming and shouting and breaking innocent people's legs.'

'I can see how you might think that. But he's a man who we all greatly respect and...'

'Look, Mr Goddard, I'm going to have to let the authorities know about all this, but I strongly advise you to get these things on the go before you are forced to do so. It will look better for you.'

'Okay.'

'I have a number of forms and leaflets out in the car; not enough for everybody here, but I see you have a photocopier so you can make a start on putting things right. I'll leave them at the gatehouse where I came in and you need to get going right away.'

'I really ought to talk about this with Elijah.'

'I suspect it's going to be a while before Elijah is able to talk about this sort of stuff. Give me your phone number and I'll give you a call in the morning to check if you've got the ball rolling.'

Paul scribbled the number on a scrap of paper. 'The phone goes through to the gatehouse. Leave a message for me there and I'll get back to you as soon as I can.'

Dr Anderton stood up. 'Right. I need to get on with my rounds now.'

Paul put out his hand to shake Dr Anderton's, but Dr Anderton ignored it.

'Liam, walk Dr Anderton back to his car and collect those forms and leaflets, will you?'

'Okay.'

'And bring them back here as soon as you can.'

Dr Anderton didn't say anything as we left the house and I was so overwhelmed with it all I couldn't think of anything to say to him either. He opened the boot of his car and handed me all the forms and leaflets that he had in there.

'Just a minute,' he said, 'give me those back.'

He searched through them and took out a few.

'You don't need the death forms… yet!'

He slammed the boot shut and walked round to the driver's door muttering, 'What a mess,' then drove off without a backward glance.

# Forty One

There was so much going on that my mind was in a whirl. Luckily Ian completely took over the gardening work, which left me free to deal with what I could.

As soon as I got back into the house, Paul asked me to go to a special meeting but, even before I got there, there was a message from the intercom into the office that the police were waiting at the gatehouse to see me. I went down there to talk to them as most of the offices seemed to be in use for one thing and another.

We sat in Paul's office and they asked me lots of questions about what had happened to Rebecca. I told them as much as I thought I could, although I didn't offer that I thought Elijah had hit her. I didn't need to bring that matter up because they did.

'So, Mr Donnelly, do you think it was Elijah who hit her?'

'I don't know. Rebecca told me she had fallen downstairs and no one was awake to see what happened so I feel I have no choice but to believe her.'

'I asked what you think, not what you know.'

'I suppose it's possible. He's never seemed to be a violent man to me but, after what I saw him doing at the hospital, I have wondered if he hit her.'

'And what about when you took her up to the hospital. We've heard that he doesn't approve of hospitals. Was there any problem before you left with Rebecca?'

'No problem at all. In fact, Elijah wasn't around when I took her in the car. No one was.'

'Was there a reason for that? Didn't you think about waking someone up before you left to say where you were going?'

'No. No, not really. I just wanted her to get medical help. Her arm seemed to be a mess.'

'So no one knew about you leaving the premises?'

'Mark was on the gatehouse, he saw us go, but I didn't tell him where we were going.'

'How did Elijah get to know where Rebecca was?'

'I rang from the hospital and told Paul. He passed the news to Elijah.'

'And that's when Elijah set off for the hospital?'

'Yes.'

'You were there when he arrived. Were you surprised when you saw how he behaved?'

'I was. Very surprised.'

'You knew he disapproved of hospitals though?'

'Err, yes, I knew.'

'Is that why you didn't tell anyone where you were going, in case they stopped you?'

The sweat was rolling down my back.

'Maybe. I didn't really think that much; I was too worried about Rebecca.'

'Right, I think we have enough for now. Could we have a word with this,' he looked at his notebook, 'Paul?'

'I think he's in a meeting.'

'Well, could you get him out of his meeting, please, this is important.'

I rang through to the house on the intercom; Gemma agreed to get Paul out of the meeting and send him down to the gatehouse. I made the police coffee while they were waiting and my hand was shaking so much I knocked the sugar over. I held my breath while I put the cups on the desk because I was so afraid I might spill it.

Through the window, I saw Paul coming down the path to the gatehouse. He looked pale.

Back in the house, George told me the meeting had been postponed until later. I suddenly realised that it was late afternoon and I hadn't had anything to eat. I wandered into the kitchen where I found Liz sat on the floor crying.

'Oh, Liz, don't cry. Everything will get sorted out.'

'It's just that the whole house is upside down and no one knows what they are supposed to do. We need Elijah. We need Rebecca. We need everybody to keep going.'

'They'll be back soon, don't you worry.'

'Do you think so?'

I didn't, at least I didn't think Elijah would be back, but now wasn't the time to mention it. 'I do.'

Liz hoisted herself up, brushed herself down and wiped her eyes.

'Now, what can I do for you? I don't suppose you're volunteering to peel potatoes?'

'I was really looking for something to eat, but if you need someone to do it ...'

'No, bless you, it will keep me busy. Will a yogurt and one of my iced buns be enough to keep you going till dinner?'

'Certainly will.'

I sat down at the kitchen table to eat and was pleased to hear Liz start singing as she began peeling the potatoes. I was glad she could push it to the back of her mind. I wished I could.

After I'd eaten, I went out to the greenhouse and worked till I heard the bell for Afternoon Assembly. It seemed a struggle but George managed to keep it like a normal service, although we ended with special prayers for Elijah and Rebecca.

Becky was downstairs for dinner for the first time that week. She waved at me from across the room, but she didn't seem to want to leave Mary's side. She didn't eat much either, but then neither did anyone else.

After dessert, Jess appeared.

'Where've you been?' I asked.

'Busy with Hanna. She's been really fussy this afternoon. I don't know whether she's teething, starting with something or if she's picking up on the atmosphere in the house. Have you seen Paul?'

'Not since this morning. Why?'

'Two things. One is that there's a meeting tonight at seven thirty. He wants you and me there. I've asked Gemma to keep an eye on Hanna for me. The other thing is that we need to go to the Registrar's tomorrow to register the babies' births. All the mothers and fathers are going. We've got special appointments with the Superintendent Registrar.'

'What time?'

'One thirty.'


When I left the dining room I went for a nap. I was exhausted so, of course, I didn't wake up in time for the meeting. Suddenly the door flung open and Jess dragged me up.

'Come on, Paul's drumming his fingers on the table waiting for you.'

I stumbled downstairs after her and down to the gatehouse office. It wasn't that big an office and it seemed packed. There was Paul, George, Rachel, Ruth, Will, Tom and Jim.

'Right, let's get going,' Paul said.

First he went over all that had happened. I had thought I knew everything but it turned out I didn't. The police had removed the car that Elijah had used to get to the hospital and taken it to Forensics. They suspected that it had been involved in knocking down a young man who was critically ill. A gasp went round the room. This was getting worse and worse.

The meeting went on for hours. We were there until after midnight. We kept going over what had happened and what might happen. We took a short break for coffee at about ten thirty. Paul and George went off somewhere to have a private word, but the rest of us stayed there. The conversation drifted in and out, sometimes we were quiet, sometimes we talked about what happened, but most of the time we tried to talk about other things, like when we had the picnic, when we had the weddings and when the babies were born.

George and Paul came back into the room and we all fell silent. They both went to the front and I noticed that George had a bundle of papers in his hand. Paul spoke first.

'George and I went off for a private word because he's brought up an idea we've discussed with Elijah before and now it seems like the way for us to go in the near future. George, do you want to tell them?'

George nodded and stood up. Paul sat down.

'As Paul said, this is an idea we've discussed with Elijah before. While we know that everyone is very happy here in this lovely house, we think it might be time for us to make a move away from here.'

There were some gasps and Tom said, almost as if he couldn't stop himself, 'You mean you want us to run away?'

'No, Tom, it's not running away. It looks to be a good way of keeping our community together. We've talked about the problems we have at the moment and we're certainly doing our best to overcome them by co-operating with the authorities. But there's still a risk. We've drawn attention to ourselves and…'

'You mean Elijah has,' muttered Will.

'Well, yes, anyway. When Elijah and Rebecca come back, we're never really going to feel secure. If there's any trouble anywhere, you can bet that we will be the first people that the police call on.'

I could see what he was saying but, still, moving away?

'Where would we go, George?' I asked

'That's where our idea comes in. We've been looking on the Internet at caravan and camping parks. We have various skills here that would fit in with such a venture. We're currently running a catering business so we could have a restaurant, maybe even carry on catering special events such as weddings. We're running a gardening business, so we could easily look after the grounds, grow our own vegetables with some left over for sale, maybe carry on selling flowers too. And, with Paul's computer skills, we could set up a website, advertise on the internet and take bookings by email. Not only that, we should have enough room for our own accommodation and worship needs.'

'And where do you think the finance is coming from?' That was Jess. Good old Jess, always looking on the practical side. 'None of us has any money. These sort of places cost big money, you know.'

That was the first time I'd ever seen Paul and George look truly uncomfortable with any situation. They looked at each other as if deciding who was to speak, then George sat down and Paul stood up.

'This is a bit awkward. There is a sum of money that we have put aside for emergencies. Quite a large sum of money as a matter of fact.'

Will asked, 'Where did it come from?'

'The bulk of it came from the money that Amy left us. We've been investing the money since then.'

Will was looking angrier and angrier, 'And the rest?'

'We put a bit by each month from our income.'

'So what sort of sum are we talking about? A few thousand?'

Paul looked down at his desk and didn't answer.

Will raised his voice. 'What sort of sum?'

'A bigger sum than that.'

Will was shouting now, 'How much?'

'Nearly two million.'

There was a gasp round the room and Will stood up, looking ready to walk out. Tom put his hand on Will's arm and persuaded him to sit down.

Will took a deep breath and spoke again. He sounded much calmer, but you could hear the anger that he was trying to keep in control.

'You mean to say that all the time we've been scrimping and saving, eating cheap meat, mending this decrepit old house to keep a roof over our heads, you've been playing about with stocks and shares, investing money like big businessmen? Using our money without discussing it with us? What sort of people are you?'

There was a lot of nodding and muttering around the room: I could sense that even the normally calm people like Tom and Jess were getting angry. I could see their point, but I'd never had anything and I didn't expect to have anything then.

'You're right,' said George, 'it is your money too. But we haven't kept it for ourselves. We've kept it as a contingency fund, that's the sensible thing to do with a big place like this.'

'How do we know you wouldn't take that money and do a runner?' Will asked. 'How do we know that you haven't been giving yourself little treats from it? Come to think of it, you always seem to have the best clothes, the best food, the best cars.'

'Oh, come on, Will, you know that's not true. We never take any more than our fair share of anything. Just take a deep breath and think about it.'

Will did take a deep breath and buried his face in his hands for a couple of minutes. We sat in silence looking at him, taking the time to get used to the way that our view of The Community had turned upside down in the past few minutes.

Will put his hands back on the table and said, shamefacedly, 'I'm sorry, I got carried away there. I know that you always want the best for us.'

'Right,' said George, 'do you all want me to go on about our plan?'

Everyone nodded and he carried on talking.

'The plan is that I'll take Liam down to Wales with me to have a look at a number of caravan parks. I think we're best leaving it till next Monday so we can avoid the weekend. No good hanging about down there when the estate agents are closed.'

I'd been shocked when I heard my name. 'Why me?'

'I don't know much about gardening and you'll be able to give me a considered opinion of the quality of the gardens that we see. The odds are that most places will have some form of catering facility that we can improve on and Paul can do his computer work pretty much anywhere. Does that sound okay, Liam?'

'Yes.' It did sound alright, but I wasn't looking forward to being without Jess and Hanna, even for a few days.

'How long will we be away?'

'It depends on how things go. I'm reckoning on about five days. Long enough to get the ball rolling when we've made our decision. When we get back we can get in touch with our solicitors to do the legal work. We know that we can trust them.'

Paul stood up. 'Everyone agreed?'

They were.

# Forty Two

We didn't get much sleep the night after the meeting. Jess was really wound up about the money, even though she hadn't said much at the meeting. She kept going on about how Elijah had only given her fifty pounds for new things for Hanna.

'Fifty pounds, that's all. Fifty pounds with two million in the bank. Two million of our money!'

'But, Jess, at least he gave you something. He didn't really have to give you, us, anything. We could have managed.'

'Why should Hanna have to do without when there's money in the bank? Why? Tell me that.'

'Jess, I'm tired. Can we talk about this in the morning? We can't do anything about it now anyway.'

'I don't care. When Elijah gets back, I'm going to have it out with him.'

'That's up to you, love, if you think it will get you anywhere. But, how's about a cuddle and going to sleep now. I won't be here next week.'

'And that's another thing. You and George gallivanting off to Wales when we could all stay here. They're just panicking, all this will blow over.'

'Jess, please. Another time. Okay? Scoot over here and let me hold you. I've had a hard day and I need some sleep.'

'You think you've had a hard day. You don't know what a hard day is. I've been up and down with Hanna, your daughter, all day long, changing nappies, talking baby talk, tickling her tummy…'

I suddenly realised she was teasing me so I pulled her to me and turned out the light. Just before I drifted off to sleep, I heard her mutter, 'Fifty pounds.'

The next morning the police were there again to talk to Paul. Everyone was taking turns going to the GPs to sign up but the couples with babies were waiting until the babies were registered. I went out on the deliveries with Ian and spent the time going over what ought to happen during the time I was away. I knew that he was perfectly capable of running things on his own, but it made me feel better to talk it over with him. He didn't mind, in fact he found it quite funny and kept bursting into laughter.

After lunch, the four couples and four babies went to the Registrars in two cars. We didn't have any baby seats for the cars so the mothers held the babies in the back. We were in with Paul and Ruth. I'd warned Jess before we left the house, but at one point I heard her mutter, 'Fifty pounds!' I glared at her and she mouthed 'Sorry,' at me.

'Everything all right, Jess?'

'Yes, thank you, Paul.'

When we all trooped into the Registrar's waiting room, it felt a little overcrowded, especially as they were another two couples in there. We had to see the Superintendent Registrar because it had been over a year since the children were born. We were given forms to fill in while we waited and then we handed them over to the receptionist.

Jess and I went in first. There was a file on the desk with Hosanna Joy Donnelly written on the front cover. We sat down facing the Superintendent Registrar, Mr Morris.

The first thing he asked was if we had received the two letters the department had sent us, warning us that we needed to register Hanna. I began to say, 'No,' but then I realised that Jess was speaking.

'Elijah tore them up. He said there was no need to register her. All that mattered was that she was a member of our community.'

217

'Then Elijah was wrong. You do need to register her. You need to register for so many reasons, including the fact that at some stage she may want to register for benefits or get herself a passport. Mr and Mrs Donnelly, do you not realise that we all need to prove our birth at some point?'

We shook our heads together and I said, 'No, I never thought about it.'

'Then perhaps you need to do a bit more thinking in the future. Now, in some ways you two are the lucky ones because at least we have a record of,' he looked down at the file, 'Hosanna Joy's birth as she was born in the hospital. We can issue a certificate without further ado.'

He filled in the name and date of birth on the certificate and then asked, 'Are you married to each other?'

'Yes,' we both said.

'Have you brought a copy of your marriage certificate?'

We didn't speak for several minutes and then Jess whispered, 'We haven't got a certificate.'

He raised one eyebrow and said, 'Oh?'

'We got married in a special ceremony at The Larches,' I told him in a trembling voice.

'Then, I'm sorry to say, you aren't legally married. It doesn't matter for Hosanna's certificate, Mr Donnelly, you can still be named on it, but it may matter at some future date.'

Deep down I'd known that we weren't legally married but I wasn't that bothered. What was important at that moment was the crisp certificate that we carried away with us, naming me as the father of little Hannah. I kept looking at it and feeling so proud.

The others were in with the Registrar for much longer than we had been. There were no records at all of the births and they were told that Social Services would have to be involved and maybe the other children would need X-rays to prove how old they were.

We called in at the GPs on the way home, again taking turns at going in. I thought the receptionist was a little sharp with me, but maybe that was my imagination.

At home, Rebecca had just returned. She looked a lot better than the last time I'd seen her, but her face was still bruised and her arm was very painful. Everyone crowded round her, making a fuss, but then Becky turned up and pushed her way through. It was lovely to see how happy she was.

# Forty Three

We left for Wales about seven in the morning. Almost before we got out of the grounds George asked, 'What's wrong with Jess?'

'Don't think anything's wrong with her. Why are you asking?'

'She seems angry about something. She keeps glaring at me.'

'Oh, that. She's angry about you keeping all that money in the bank while Elijah only gave her fifty pounds to spend on Hanna. She thinks the money should have been used to make life easier for all of us.'

'Well, I can see her point, but we decided early on .we needed to have contingency funds because we never knew what our future was. It's like an insurance policy. Paul dealt with the investments; he's good at things like that, although we never expected it to grow into such a large amount. Do you think we did wrong?'

'I don't know. I can see Jess's point and I can see yours and I can't decide between them.'

'Good old Liam. Always the diplomat.'

I don't think I was being diplomatic, but it seemed that I'd totally lost the ability to make decisions. I'd gone into a sort of dreamlike state where everything passed in front of my eyes and I didn't seem to have any control over it. The countryside rushed by and my mind couldn't grab hold and make sense of anything; it was all a jumble.

Not only that, it hurt every minute I moved further away from Jess and Hanna. Only that pain seemed real and the sooner we'd done what we set out to do, the better.

We were booked at a hotel in Aberystwyth and, as we arrived before checking in time, George insisted that we visit the estate agent that looked most promising.

I would have preferred a walk along the seafront. I wasn't feeling at my best. Some of it was car sickness; I wasn't used to travelling so far and there were all the hills that we went up and down on our journey. Plus there'd been that greasy bacon sandwich that George insisted I had, even though we had enough food for the whole community in the car; Liz was worried we'd be hungry.

George was acting like he was on holiday, he whistled and sang as he drove and, every time we stopped, he'd climb out of the car and say, 'Smell that fresh air.' All I could smell was petrol fumes.

The estate agent had two caravan parks on its books. One was up and running, the other had been closed for over twelve months and 'needed a bit of work.'

'Any chance we could view them both this afternoon,' George asked.

The estate agent looked at his watch. 'I should think so. I'm afraid I can't go with you, but I can give you the keys for the closed one and I'll call Mr Peters at the other one to expect you. Have you got a sat nav?'

We must have looked blank at him (we know what they are now; we watched a programme on TV while we were staying at the hotel.)

'Never mind, I'll lend you a couple of maps.'

The open one was the nearest, about five miles away from Aberystwyth centre. The journey was easy, not much traffic on the road and we arrived very quickly. The owner was looking out for us and came out to greet us as we were parking up.

'Mr Jamieson and Mr Donnelly?'

'That's right,' said George as he took the man's outstretched hand.

'I'm Mr Peters,' he said, shaking my hand too. His hand was slightly damp and I felt that he wasn't as relaxed as he seemed. I didn't like him, but couldn't quite put my finger on it.

He took us on what he called 'the grand tour'. It seemed quiet to me, but he explained that away by saying it was out of season. I was out of touch with holiday seasons but I would have expected September to be a little busier than that.

There was a large central building holding a reception desk, a bar, cafe with kitchen behind, shop and a club room, which was used for all sorts of events, from children's entertainment to the 'occasional lap dancing night for the locals.' George raised his eyebrows at that.

Everywhere looked like it needed a good clean, but I knew that wasn't a problem for us; plenty of willing workers where we came from. Mr Peters took us out of the back door and across a dirt track to the owner's house. It looked quite modern but, when we got inside, it was pretty depressing: the kitchen was covered with dirty pots and pans and the furniture and curtains were scruffy and uncared for.

'Sorry, didn't have time to clean up before you got here. The missus, well, she left me a couple of months ago and I've let things get on top of me.'

'Must have been difficult for you,' George said, looking sympathetic.

Next he showed us one of the ten static caravans. 'Half of these are privately owned—we manage the rental for them and the rest are ours.'

He took us inside one of them. Here again, it looked like it needed a good clean. Outside again, we walked round the grounds: a children's play area, a paddling pool without water, 'too cold,', space for another twenty touring caravans and fifteen tents, a shower block and, the thing that grabbed my interest, a separate large garden, which had obviously once been well cared for but was now neglected.

'Is there a chance of looking at your books, Mr Peters?' George asked.

'Certainly.'

'Liam, do you want to have a better look round the garden?'

I nodded, too busy thinking about what I could do in there to talk. I don't know how long they were away because I was busy scribbling notes in the notebook I'd brought specially. A man, who turned out to be the handyman, came and asked what I was doing.

'We're thinking about buying it,' I said, 'I would be running the garden side.'

'Was a good little business in its day, but he's let it go since his wife left.'

'Yes, Mr Peters mentioned his wife wasn't here anymore.'

I wanted to get on with things, but this man obviously wanted to pass on the gossip.

'He got involved with one of the lap dancers. She moved in with him for a while but it didn't work out, he wanted her to do all the cleaning as well as keep up with the lap dancing to bring the money in. Since she left he's let everything go. Business is well down.'

'Really?'

'Yes, we lost the family trade because of the lap dancing, then we lost the lap dancing so the locals stopped coming. He's in debt up to his eyes.'

'George is dealing with the business side. He's looking at the books now.'

'Well, I wouldn't trust old Peters as far as I could throw him, you mark my words.'

He wandered off and I carried on with my plans. Later, back in the car, George said, 'It has possibilities, that's for sure. Need to beat him down on the price, but that's probably going to be true for all of them.'

I told him what the handyman had said.

'Is that so? If we decide to go for this one, then I'll get our accountant to go over those books for me before we make an offer'.

Next we went to the closed caravan park. After battling our way through a series of locked gates and padlocks, we found ourselves in a big untidy space containing about five ancient caravans, but with room for a lot more. There was an enormous, two storey building ahead of us, some of the windows were broken but otherwise it looked in decent condition.

Inside we found that, downstairs, it held the same sort of rooms as in the previous one, the only difference being that everything was a lot bigger. The stairs were behind a locked door marked 'Private' but we soon found the right key and went upstairs to have a look.

I felt at home as soon I put my foot on the top step. I don't know why. Maybe it was the light that flooded in to the large kitchen, even though it was late afternoon. Maybe it was the worn but cosy looking sofas that filled the living room. Maybe it was just the spacious feel that reminded me of The Larches. Whatever it was, I wanted to stay.

'It's certainly got potential. We wouldn't have to have people living in here, they could have caravans outside. Not only that, because it isn't a going concern, we could take our time making it suitable for us and then open it up as a holiday park. No need to worry about outstanding bookings.'

There were more buildings outside; including a large barn which George thought could be an Assembly Room. I was getting worried, though; there didn't seem to be a garden that could be used for me to set up a business. George, sat on a bench to go over the particulars, noticed a section at the back saying the market garden next door might be available for sale by separate negotiation. We couldn't spot it where we were so we went back into the main building and looked out of the windows.

'I think that's it,' I said, 'behind that locked gate.'

We went down and had a look. We couldn't find the key for the gate so I climbed over it; a bit worried I might get caught, but too keen to see it to wait. It was great, just the right size for our business and even bigger than the one at the Larches. I'd made my decision already, although I didn't mention it to George.


We ate dinner in the hotel and then went for a drive down to the seafront. We parked up and decided to go for a walk in the evening air. The sun was setting and the sky was full of pinks and greys. I loved it.

George started talking. 'What do you think, Liam? Do you think we could make a go of this move?'

'I think so. The caravan park seems a good idea if we can afford to buy one and run it.'

'We aren't going to be looking at any we can't afford. Of course, there'll be setting up costs and if we go for one like the second one we saw today then we'll have a lot of expense but, of course, the need for that will be reflected in the asking price.'

'I'll miss The Larches though.'

'So will I.'

'Do we have to move?

'Looks like we've been painted into a corner. We've drawn attention to ourselves big style. Even though we're scurrying round trying to jump through all the hoops they're setting up for us, there'll never be a time when we can feel as secure as we have been doing. And if Elijah is sent to prison...'

'Do you think he will be?'

'It's looking that way, although, judging from the way he's been behaving, it may be that they extend the section that's keeping him in the hospital and he may never be declared sane enough for a trial.'

'Is he really as bad as that?'

'He is. I went up to see him yesterday afternoon. I stayed over an hour and he didn't talk a word of sense the entire time I was there. I'm very worried about him and there's nothing we can do to help him. It looks like, whether or not we move, we're going to need a new Community Leader.'

'I can't imagine our community without Elijah as our Leader.'

'Neither can I.'

That wasn't strictly true. I'd often thought about how things would be if Elijah wasn't in charge. How I wouldn't have to listen to him ranting on. How I wouldn't have to worry about Jess and him, even though she always said she wasn't interested. How there might be less chopping and changing to our routines. But, even so, change is always difficult, even though you think it's for the better.


We stayed in Wales for another three days, visiting sites around Aberaeron, New Quay and Cardigan. They fell into the two groups we'd seen with the first two; either open and run down or closed and absolutely ramshackle.

We also did a lot of talking and came to the conclusion that the second one we saw, the closed caravan site, was the one for us. George went back to the estate agent alone to negotiate. I was glad about that. I didn't want involving in any of the financial side of it all. My garden business was enough finance for me to deal with; I couldn't help with any more than that.

So, I was on my own in what was really a strange place. I wandered down to the Promenade and walked along, watching all the holidaymakers. I wished Jess and Hanna were there. I could imagine what Hanna's face would be like if she ever saw the sea. I wanted to talk to Jess. I wanted to hear Hanna say, 'Dada'. I wanted to hear home. Since we left, the days had been long and dreamlike, the nights had gone on for ever; the sound of George's snuffling and snoring grated on my ears and stopped me sleeping. If I could have rung Jess and Hanna, I would have, but it wasn't possible. We'd already rung the gatehouse to leave messages for Paul, but I couldn't leave one for Jess; that wasn't how it worked.

I sat on a bench and thought about going in a bar. Just for one drink. But I made myself stay where I was. I tried to stop myself thinking and concentrated on watching what was going on around me. The waves rolled up on the sand and rolled back out again. The holiday makers walked past with hot dogs, bags of chips and cups of what I had learned were called cappuccinos and lattes. Children ran away from their parents and were scolded until they went back again. Time passed by without my noticing it.

'We did it,' a voice said in my ear, making me jump. I turned. It was George. 'I beat them down by ten thousand. Did a great deal. It was just like the old days.'

'That's brilliant. Are you going to ring The Larches?'

'No, I thought we'd tell them when we get back. Make it more of an event.'

'So when *are* we going back.'

'Bit late to go back now so we'll make it first thing in the morning. Set the alarm for six and have an early start.'

I didn't see why we couldn't go then, but I didn't like to say so. 'Sounds good to me.'

'Why don't we go for a drink to celebrate?'

'No, George, I shouldn't. I mustn't.'

'Oh, it will be alright. You can have a coke.'

We went into a pub on the front. George pushed his way to the bar and I trailed along behind him.

'Vodka and coke, please. No, wait a minute, make it two.'

'No, George, please.'

'One won't do you any harm.'

My head was screaming 'no,' but my voice said, 'okay'.

George was talking about the deal, telling me about the phone calls and the negotiating but I couldn't really take it in. I was in turmoil; the temptation to have another vodka, and another, was pulling me apart. I was about to go to the bar to order another for us both when I saw, through the window, a woman carrying a baby. It looked like Jess and Hanna. This had to stop.

George pushed his chair back. 'I'm going to get another. Want one?'

'I'll go,' I said and went to the bar where I bought vodka for him and a coke for me. I made my coke last so he didn't offer to get me another drink. He got himself two more vodka and cokes.

My one alcoholic drink had hit me quite hard. I hadn't had a drink for a long time; I felt more relaxed and didn't really worry about George drinking so much. At least, I didn't worry for a while.

'I've always liked you, Liam. You've made a grand job of that gardening business and you and Jess, well, a marriage made in heaven.'

'Thanks, George.'

'And that little baby of yours, she's the prettiest baby in the house. I mean that, I really do. And smart. She's so smart. You should be proud of her, really, really proud.'

'I am.'

'Tell me, Liam, do you love Jess, really love her?'

'Yes, George, I love her. Think maybe we should be…'

'I was worried when Elijah put you two together. I wasn't sure you'd be a good match. I mean, Jess is so clever and you, well, you're not stupid, I'm not saying that, but you're not the brightest star in the sky. Not got a lot of education, have you?'

'No, George, I haven't got a lot of education, but don't you think we…'

'See, I thought Jess would lack intellectual stimulation and be unhappy with you, but maybe you're making up for it in other areas, hey?'

He dug his elbow into my ribs and nearly fell off his chair. He pulled himself upright and repeated, 'Other areas,' before laughing really loudly.

'Come on, George, time to go,' I said, standing up and putting my arm under his armpit to make him stand.

'Can't we have another? One more for the road?'

'No, we've got an early start tomorrow, remember?'

'Oh, yes, early start. Good news to pass on.'

The fresh air outside cleared my head completely but it made George worse. He staggered all over the place and muttered to himself virtually all the way to the hotel. It was only when we were in the hotel car park that he stood up tall, looked me in the eye and said, 'Pray he doesn't do it.'

'Pray who doesn't do what?' I asked, more in the way of wanting to keep him calm rather than anything else.

'Pray Elijah doesn't do what he told me; escape from the hospital and send everyone off to a better life in heaven. It's not their time yet, it's not their time!'

# Forty Four

I didn't sleep well. I was all churned up inside worrying about what George had said, worrying about Jess and Hanna up in that house where that madman might turn up at any time and, somehow, persuade them all that suicide was the way to go. If it hadn't been for the fact that I knew Elijah was in a secure ward, I might have bundled George into the car and driven back home straight away.

George had told me about the locked doors and windows on the ward and how no patient could get out without being seen. Even Elijah wouldn't have the ability to get out of that, especially when he was in such a state and he was sedated as well. I calmed myself as much as I could and eventually drifted off to sleep. I probably got about two hours before the alarm went off.

I tried to wake George, but he wasn't having any of it. He kept pushing me away. I went downstairs, ate a bit of breakfast and then went to the room to try again. The panic was back and I wanted to get on the road as soon as possible.

He was still snoring loudly. I shook his shoulder and shouted his name, but it had no effect at all. I packed the bags, putting out clean clothes for George (he'd slept in his) and took the bags down to the car. When I got back to the room, I went to the sink, filled a glass with cold water and poured it over his head.

'What the… Liam, for God's sake, what's got into you?'

'We've got to go, George, we've got to go.'

'Alright, alright. Let me come round a bit and pack and…'

'I've packed, the bags are in the car and your clean clothes are here. Get yourself washed and dressed.'

It was about another hour before we got on the road. George sat in the back and went to sleep. We had a flat tyre at Bala which I changed on my own while George carried on snoring in the car. Then there were roadworks somewhere, can't remember where, and I became more and more agitated as I waited in the traffic.

It was late evening before we got into Lancashire. We stopped at a supermarket for George to use the toilets. He was wide awake now but not in a good mood, grumbling at everything; the brightness of the lights, the smell of the burger place, the noise of the slot machines.

On our way out, I spotted a pile of Lancashire Evening Telegraphs with the headline, 'Local Preacher Escapes From Secure Psychiatric Ward.'

# Forty Five

*Local Preacher Escapes From Secure Psychiatric Ward*

Local Preacher, Robert Ellis, also known as Elijah, has escaped from a secure ward at the Royal Blackburn Hospital where he has been kept under sedation since causing a disturbance in the A & E unit after his wife, Rebecca, was admitted last week. It is suspected that Mr Ellis caused the injuries for which she was admitted.

The police have been trying to interview Mr Ellis, not only about the disturbance, but also about an incident with a car driven by Mr Ellis which left Mr Gregory Hallam injured at the roadside. Mr Ellis failed to stop and, as Mr Hallam subsequently died from his injuries, it is expected that Mr Ellis will be charged with manslaughter when he is fit to do so.

It appears that Mr Ellis had been pretending to take his medication, but has not done so, hiding the pills in his bedside cabinet. He stole some outdoor clothes from another patient and, having dressed in said clothes, mingled with a group of visitors as they left the ward.

He does not appear to have returned to The Larches, which houses the religious community led by Mr Ellis. The police advise anyone who sees him not to approach him, but to call them immediately

No one at The Larches was available for comment.

# Forty Six

It was late evening when we got to The Larches, the gate was padlocked and the building was in darkness. I'd never seen it like that. George tried his keys, but none of them worked on the padlock. We prowled round the boundary fencing until we found a spot where we could work it loose and squeeze through.

The doors into the house were locked too. This was not good. My heart was pounding and my mouth was dry. I urgently wanted a drink; not necessarily alcohol, although it crossed my mind.

'Are you thinking what I'm thinking?' asked George, searching through his pockets for the keys he'd had only a minute earlier.

I nodded. Then wished I hadn't. Some things are so awful you can't allow yourself to think they are possible.

He found the front door key and fit it into the lock. It turned, but the door wouldn't open.

'They must have put the bars on. Let's try the kitchen door.'

We went round to the back. It was fully dark by now and I kept imagining I saw someone following us. I was scared, really scared and I hoped we'd got back in time.

We managed to open the kitchen door after a lot of pushing. The bar on that door was pretty flimsy. We put the light on and gasped at the state of the kitchen. There were pots and pans scattered everywhere with dirty plates piled up on the sink and the work surfaces. We shouted, 'Hello,' but only silence answered us. We looked at each other.

'Cellar,' we both said at the same time. I don't know about George, but I was torn in two by that word. I wanted to look, I wanted to find out but, at the same time, I didn't want to know because, if I knew for sure, my life would be over.

George got the key from his desk. We went through the kitchen, into the pantry and unlocked the cellar door. There was a toy car on the steps. At the bottom, we unlocked the door and pushed. It stuck so we pushed harder to make a gap we could get through.

Inside the kitchen we found what had been blocking the door. It was Methuselah. From the scratches on the back of the door, it seemed that he'd tried to escape, but couldn't get out. There was a trickle of blood running from his nose and his body was quite cold.

George's breathing was loud, but I didn't seem to be breathing at all. My chest was tight; I wanted to run back up those stairs and away from there. I put my hand on the wall to steady myself and looked round the kitchen. There were several cups out on the worktop and some of those big metal water jugs like we used to have at school. There was a puddle of coloured liquid next to one of the jugs and I put my finger out to taste it.

'Don't,' shouted George, 'it might be poison.'

Part of me had known that but somehow the liquid had drawn me to it.

'Come on,' said George, 'let's get it over with.'

We went to the Assembly Room. Another locked door but this one opened easily with the key. And there it was. My nightmare come true. A room full of the people I loved and cared for; some sitting bolt upright, others curled up on the floor. All dead. There was a baby in the centre, sitting on someone's knee, facing the door; eyes still open and staring straight at me.

'Hanna?' I shouted. I held out my arms to her, watched for her to put her arms up in the air, asking for me to pick her up. She didn't move. I tried to get to her, but there were all these people in the way; all these bodies in the way.

234

'Hanna,' I shouted again.

George put his hand on my shoulder.

'Liam, it's not her. She's not here.'

'Are you sure? Are you absolutely positive?'

'It's Adah. Definitely Adah. Look again.'

I rubbed my eyes. It *was* Adah, sitting on Gemma's knee. I tried to look around for Jess, but my eyes weren't working at all now, I couldn't seem to focus.

'And Jess? Can you see Jess?'

'She's not here either. I promise you, Liam, she's not here. But, maybe next door, they might be in there.'

I pushed my way out and into the next room, the Social Room. There was another baby in there; little Joe still held tight in Andrea's arms. I reached out, touched his face. It was cold. A kind of cold I'd never touched before. His bottle was on the floor, half-filled with that green liquid that we'd seen in the kitchen.

I looked at George.

'They're definitely not in here either,' he said.

'Do you think they are alright?'

'I hope so. We need to look round the rest of the cellar, to be sure there's no one else here and then look round the house. There's other people missing: Rebecca, Becky, Ruth, Emmanuel, Jonathan, Gideon, maybe some others. It's hard to work out exactly who is and isn't here.'

He was right. The horror of those two rooms stopped me thinking logically and, with a community of sixty people, it was too long a list to remember all the names at a time like this.

We looked round the cellar. There was definitely no one else there. We went up the stairs and closed the door behind us.

'We can't do anything for those poor souls,' George said, 'We need to look for the living.'

That feeling of being watched was back again and, as we crossed the pantry towards the kitchen door, I felt someone behind me. It was Elijah with a kitchen knife raised towards my back. I grabbed his wrist and held the knife up in the air.

'Where are they, Elijah, where's Jess and Hanna? Are they still alive?'

He was struggling with me, trying to get the knife free. George reached up to take the knife from Elijah's hand but it was too high for him to reach so he took hold around Elijah's waist and tried to pull him over.

'Come on, Elijah; tell us where the others are and if they are still alive.'

'If I knew where they were, they wouldn't be alive. It's time for us all to leave this earth, time for us to set up our community in a higher place, with God.'

He pulled his arm free from me and swung the knife down in an arc which caught George's shoulder. Moving quicker than I thought possible George took hold of the knife with his other hand and spun it across the room. Elijah dropped to his knees and tried to scramble after it, but I flung myself onto his back and held him. George was holding on to his arm which was bleeding heavily.

'What are we going to do with him?' I asked.

'The only thing I can think of is to lock him in the cellar.'

It took every ounce of strength I had to hold Elijah still while George opened the doors then we manhandled Elijah down the stairs, pushed him into the kitchen and tried to close the door. He kept pushing it back open before we could lock it and, in the end, I wedged my feet against the bottom step so I could lean against the door and provide enough force to get that door closed while George locked it. We raced back up the steps and locked the cellar door. Then we left the pantry, closed the door and tied the handle to the radiator.

'That should certainly hold him for a while, but in the state he's in I wouldn't be sure that any door can hold him.'

I set off through the kitchen.

'Liam, where are you going?'

'I'm looking for Jess and Hanna.'

'Let's do it calmly and logically, together.'

I wanted to run round the house, shouting and screaming their names but George moved slowly and carefully, holding my arm all the time. Each room we went into was a mess, chairs overturned and cupboard doors left open.

'Elijah's been here before us, searching for anyone who escaped,' George said.

Upstairs, he let me go off on my own, up into the attic. I went to our room first. It was empty. The cot was untidy; looking like someone had grabbed the sheets and blankets up in a hurry. Hanna's favourite rabbit, the one that she always slept next to, was missing.

I lost the will to rush round in that room. I wanted to take things slow, look for clues. I searched through the drawers, but there was nothing. Then I remembered that Jess sometimes used to leave notes for me under my pillow. I lifted the pillow up and there was a scrap of paper with the word 'barn' scrawled on it in Jess's writing.

I raced down the stairs as fast as I could, shouting, 'George, George.' He came out and must have known from my face that this wasn't the time for talking. He followed me down the next set of stairs, out of the house and down towards the barn. It was very dark and we both stumbled several time before we got there.

Yet another locked door. I banged on the door, yelling, 'Jess.' After what seemed like hours she opened it slowly, but, when she saw my face she flung it backwards and stepped into my arms.

237

'You're alright,' I said, 'you're alright. I was so worried, so scared.'

'Me too.'

'Where's Hanna?'

She turned and pointed. Hanna was in a makeshift bed on the floor with Emmanuel, the two of them sleeping soundly. The others came forward: Rebecca, Becky, Ruth, Jonathan, Gideon, Mary and Will.

'Is this all the people who escaped?'

'Yes,' said Jess, 'everyone else followed Paul into the cellar. We'd had an Assembly where Elijah and Paul talked about how it was a special day, how it was time to make our journey to heaven and leave this wicked world behind.'

'I didn't believe them,' said Ruth, 'I didn't want anything to happen to Emmanuel. Paul knew what I felt; we'd often talked about it. I made my views clear to him, but Paul, being Paul, his first loyalty was to Elijah, although I think he didn't want Emmanuel to die either. When I said I was going to get Emmanuel from his cot, I could see in his eyes that he didn't want me to bring him down.'

Jess went on, 'Elijah ran round the house, shouting and screaming for everyone to come out. Those of us who knew that something was about to happen, had already agreed to make for the upstairs office; the door has a strong lock on it. At the end, Elijah realised we were in there. He banged and shouted for us to come out, but we kept very quiet and, eventually, he went away. We thought it was a trick so we waited a while, but when he didn't come back we made our way down to the barn. We knew we could hide in the loft there if he came looking.'

Jess suddenly stopped talking and looked at me with tearful eyes.

'Did it happen? Did they do it?'